DUSTY AYRES AND HIS BATTLE BIRDS:
CRIMSON DOOM

CRIMSON DOOM

By Robert Sidney Bowen

ALTUS PRESS • 2017

EDITED AND DESIGNED BY

Matthew Moring

PUBLISHING HISTORY

"Crimson Doom" originally appeared in the August, 1934 (Vol. 6, No. 1) issue of *Dusty Ayres and his Battle Birds* magazine. Copyright 2017 by Steeger Properties, LLC. All rights reserved.

CHAPTER 1
HELL'S TRUCE

THE MAP was about twelve feet long by five feet high, and took up most of the rear wall space of the Group office. Its glossy surface was almost completely covered with colored pins, lengths of knitting wool and innumerable pencil and ink markings. So much so, in fact, that it would require at least two good looks to realize that it was a topographical map of the U.S. Canada border from Winnipeg to the Bay of Fundy, extending north to Hudson Bay, and south to the Chicago end of Lake Michigan.

In front of the map, feet spread wide and hands jammed in tunic pockets, stood Dusty Ayres, ranking speed eagle of Uncle Sam's brood, and officially rated as flight skipper of High Speed Group Number Seven.

At his side stood Major Drake, C.O. of the Group. Both were staring at the map.

Presently the C.O. cursed softly, and broke the silence which had existed for a full three minutes.

"I'd give my right arm to know definitely," he stated, "what move those devils plan next!"

The pilot grunted, and looked at the C.O.

"It's my guess that it's going to be soon. They haven't made a move against us for ten days. Not since we gave them their first trimming at Duluth. And if the way they crashed through

"DUSTY" AYRES

Asia and Europe means anything, it's not a policy of the Black Invaders to wait very long between blows."

"Exactly!" the other broke in savagely. "Why haven't they struck again? Why have they allowed us to place our guns practically hub to hub from Duluth to the southern tip of the Great Lakes and up to the northern part of Maine?

"Over four million American soldiers!" he said. "Complete with guns, tanks, aircraft and all the rest of it. And up here—"

He paused long enough to trace another circular line from Duluth north to Hudson Bay and down across New Brunswick.

"At least the same number of Black Invaders! Yet, outside of their mopping up what was left of the Canadian Home Defense army, they haven't done a damned thing. I wish to God I knew what they are waiting for!"

Dusty nodded but said nothing.

War! Only ten days of it thus far. That is, as far as the United States was concerned. But the rest of the world had been steeped in it for three long years.

In Central Asia it had found its beginning. From out of that whirlpool of mixed bloods had arisen a man of mystery—a figure who was soon to become known as Fire-Eyes, Emperor of the World. No one had ever seen his face, for it was always covered with a green mask, perfectly blank save for two slits through which orbs of sparkling flame looked out on the world. The rest of his body, every single part of it, was covered by a black uniform. Even black gauntlets for the hands, and a black skull cap that extended down over the back of the neck.

Without warning, his fierce and cruel armies, who became known as the Black Invaders, had started sweeping across the world, crushing everything that civilized man had built up since the beginning of time. In three years all Europe and Asia was ground beneath the iron heel of Fire-eyes.

And next—the greatest nation of all, the United States of America.

The first blow against it had been a surprise one struck just ten days ago. High speed air transports had carried the Invaders secretly into the wilds of northern Ontario, and their surprise attempt to drive a steel wedge straight down through the central part of the United States had come within an ace of being a success.

Only by the grace of God and a fighting heart had the Americans been able to thwart the effort, and drive the enemy back across the Canadian line. A key man in that great defense had been Dusty Ayres.

He nodded now, as he sensed the C.O.'s eyes fixed on him questioningly.

"I agree with you, sir," he said slowly. "There must be something extra big behind it all. I have the hunch that they're waiting for something."

"What?" the word came out like a pistol shot.

Dusty shrugged.

"Damned if I know!"

Major Drake snorted, doubled his right fist and twisted it into the palm of his other hand.

"If only Washington would cut it out!" he said tersely.

"Meaning what, sir?"

"Stop playing this blasted waiting game, too!" growled Drake.

And with a savage nod he stiff-legged over to a window and stood staring moodily out across spring-painted, rolling hills that stretched westward from the Group's new base at Worcester, Massachusetts.

In silence Dusty joined him. But neither had eyes for the beauties of nature. As a matter of fact they both stared and saw nothing. Their thoughts were to the northward, up where murdering hordes crouched ready to spring at most any moment. **AND THEN,** suddenly, the door flew open and a red-faced radio corporal burst inside, waving a message.

"Just came through, sir!" he panted. "I sent an orderly to tell the Group sergeant to make ready with the planes. Guess it means something, sir, huh?"

The C.O. didn't answer. With a quick movement he smoothed out the form, glanced at the teletyped words. Dusty read it over his shoulder, and sucked in his breath sharply. The message read:

EMERGENCY... ALL NORTHEASTERN AIR BASES.

Take air at once and search for Seventh Attack Group plane number AT-8. This high altitude ship is manned by an enemy pilot, it is believed, and left Washington base drome at eight forty-five. Believe plane is following coast northward. If plane is sighted, force it to land... DO NOT SHOOT IT DOWN! All pilots will report individually on progress to Washington base over wave-lengths 205-230. Remember, do not shoot plane down... force pilot to land and surrender.

Signed, Bradley, U.S.A.F.

"From the big boy, himself!" breathed Dusty. "I wonder what the—"

He didn't finish. Major Drake had leaped across the room and jabbed one of the signal buttons that lined the right edge of his desk. From atop the roof of the Group office a siren was wailing out its call.

"Your guess is as good as mine," said the C.O. as he made for the door. "I can't figure it either. But at least it's something different to do. Never mind takeoff formation. Get into the air and keep your eyes open."

The last was unnecessary. Dusty had already barged past him through the door, and was pounding ground across the field to the third hangar. Even as he reached it, Group greaseballs dollied his plane out onto the tarmac, nose to the wind.

It was a sight for any airman's eyes, that plane. The Silver Flash, Dusty had christened it, and it lived up to its name. It was the fastest thing known to the aeronautical world, and without trying extra hard, Dusty had hung up an all-time straightaway speed mark of 527 m.p.h. But for the coming of war he would have eventually bettered that mark by an extra 50 m.p.h.

But as he leaped into its up-to-the-minute fitted cockpit, he wasn't thinking of world speed records. True, a wave of joy flooded through him as the old familiar instrument board met his eyes, and he felt the snugness of the bucket seat. He always did feel that way when he was in the Silver Flash. It was part of him, that sky chariot—a sort of something that was his and his alone. Without it, he'd be like a man without arms or legs.

For one fleeting second he ran his hand affectionately along the grooved cockpit rim, then whipped the hand to the ignition switch, and toed down on the electric starter.

A giant whine, and then the variable pitch, hollow steel propeller spun over and sent sunlight flickering off into space. Releasing the wheel brake for an instant he goosed the ship out onto the edge of the field. Then he braked, raised his right hand and glanced at the signal officer atop the signal tower on the center hangar.

As the orange flag swooped down he heeled the throttle all the way forward. Like a dart from a blow-gun, the Silver Flash streaked across a dozen yards or more of hard ground and then soared heavenward, the twenty-five hundred horses under its cowled nose roaring a full-throated song of unlimited power.

Holding the nose up, Dusty swung due east, adjusted his radio headphones, and snapped on the dash panel set. Twisting the wave-length dial reading to Washington 207, he put his lips to the transmitter tube.

"Ayres, H.S. Seven calling Washington. Headed east for Boston at twenty-five thousand. Any reports or orders?"

The earphones crackled human sound in his ears.

"No reports so far. Hold course and patrol Area K-Two-Zero-Six until satisfied… Signing off."

As the set went dead, Dusty turned the roller strip map attached to the instrument board, and found Area K-206. A grunt slipped off his lips. K-206 was a hundred square miles of Atlantic ocean due east of Cape Cod.

"Okay," he murmured to himself, sliding closed the glass cockpit cowl. "It's fishing you go then, Dusty, old sock."

THUNDERING EASTWARD to Boston, he killed time by mulling the Washington emergency message over in his mind. But he didn't get very far with his imagination. As a matter of fact the order, "Do Not Shoot Down This Plane," stopped him like a brick wall. What in hell was the idea of that? Hadn't the ship been obviously swiped? Wasn't there a Black pilot at the controls?

The last caused him to stiffen, and his eyes to go hard. Could it be that perhaps the Black Hawk, himself, was that pilot? The Black Hawk, top vulture of the Black Invaders!

Before the raid on Duluth he'd crossed props with that eagle killer. He had hoped that his guns really had finished the Hawk when they met for the second time as the Invaders retreated from Duluth. A sea of fire had swallowed up the Hawk, and he hadn't seen him again. But—

His grip on the spade handle of the stick tightened and his knuckles went white.

"If he is alive," he got out from between tight lips, "I'll damn well make sure next time."

Sweeping out over Boston Harbor, and past the tip of Cape Cod, he throttled a bit and slid down toward open water far below. Ten minutes of that and he started climbing back up again in ever-widening circles.

As he reached twenty thousand, there was a muffled clicking in the earphones. He knew instantly that it was some small sea station speaking on a wave-length that overlapped his own.

With his free hand he turned on full reception power, set the directional finder, and slowly regulated the tuning dial.

It was a matter of almost a minute before he could get anything clear. And even then it was "fuzzy" in spots. But he didn't care about that. The blood was dancing excitedly through his veins.

The sender was aboard a U.S. Navy patrol cruiser, and talking with Washington Navy Department. As the message was repeated, Dusty strained his ears to make sure that he had heard correctly.

"Cruiser Nine Forty-two to Washington. Our detectors have picked up American engine traveling high northwest by west. Our position sixty-eight-thirty, forty-one-thirty. Suggest you check on this craft regarding Air Force emergency order picked up by this station. Signing off for M.R. signal."

Even as the "message received" signal crackled out to that cruiser operator, Dusty was heeling home the throttle and tearing around to the northwest. A glance at his position map and a bit of rapid calculation had set his nerves quivering at peak pitch.

Assuming that the "phantom" plane was the one in question, and assuming that it held its present course, he should be able to cross its path just south of the lower tip of Nova Scotia.

True, he had no way of telling for sure at what altitude the plane would fly. But by assuming that the phantom plane was the plane, he could make a damned good guess.

The Seventh Attack Group ships got their best speed out of their Tandem Diesels at between twenty-five and thirty thousand feet. In all probability the Black pilot knew the ship he was flying, and would therefore travel between those two levels.

The more he thought of it, the more Dusty was positive that luck was his, and that he'd got the "smoke" of his quest. For one thing, a land plane wouldn't be that far out at sea.

For another, if it was a Navy plane it would have picked up the cruiser's message and immediately flashed down the correction.

And thirdly, and most convincing of all, how would a Black fly from Washington to his own base in Canada? Up the coast as reported? Like hell he would, unless he was thick from the boots up. He'd start along the coast then swing out to sea, veer northward and cut back in over the top of Maine.

Hardly realizing that he was doing it, he nodded his head in complete agreement with his flash deductions. And then suddenly he snorted aloud.

"Hold it, braintrust!" he grunted. "Suppose that all your theories are okay, and you meet him—then what? Your orders are to force him down. Yeah, and what if he happens to be nasty enough not to be forced?"

In answer to the last question, he spun the wave-length dial to standard pursuit plane reading.

"Ayres, H.S. Seven. Have intercepted ship-to-shore message about unidentified plane flying northwest by west course toward Area P-six. Headed for that position myself. Suggest that planes near that area change course and converge on that point. Ayres, signing off."

A sense of duty-done flooding through him, he stuck the nose of the Silver Flash up a bit and hunched forward over the stick. It was just a question of time. In fact, a question of minutes.

A quick glance at the dash watch and the ground-speed calculator showed him that it was a matter of exactly twenty-three minutes.

Twenty-three minutes. An eternity dragged by. And then Dusty saw it.

It was just a tiny dot, a pinpoint silhouetted against a billowy cloud far off his right quarter. Seconds whipped past, the dot grew larger, took on the definite shape and outline of an attack plane.

And then, as it seemed to swerve away from him, a shaft of

sunlight skidded off the glossy side of its fuselage. Painted on the side of that fuselage was the marking, AT-8!

CHAPTER 2
KIDNAP PATROL

A T-8! TEARING his eyes from the plane for an instant, he made a quick search of the surrounding heavens. He saw nothing but blue air and drifting clouds. He grabbed up the transmitter tube.

"Ayres speaking. Have spotted missing ship in Area P-Six. Closing in on it immediately. Assistance needed if possible. Signing off."

Even as he reached out his free hand to the dial knob, the red panel bug-light flickered frantically, and a sharp voice blasted against his eardrums.

"Captain Ayres… Captain Ayres, Washington H.Q. speaking. Picked up your message. Do the best you can, but do not shoot down that plane. Repeat… do not shoot down that plane. Keeping wave-length clear for report on progress."

Dusty started to rap words into the transmitter, then changed his mind. Hell, what was the sense of asking questions now? Explanations could come later. The stolen plane was veering sharply to the north. That meant the unknown pilot had either seen him, or intercepted his message.

Realization of that fact brought a worried frown to his brows. Damn Washington! Why had they crackled that "don't shoot down" order out over the air?

If that mystery pilot had overheard it, he could just sit pretty and laugh at him. How in hell could you make a bird go down when he knew damned well that you'd received orders not to shoot him down?

With a snort, Dusty ruddered after the fleeing ship and gave the Silver Flash everything it could take. And that was more than enough.

Like a streamlined transcontinental limited overtaking a slow electric freight, the Silver Flash whammed down on the attack ship.

Slipping both thumbs up to the electric trigger trips, he sent a short burst from his twin Brownings whining across the top wing of the other ship. But its pilot did not change his course an inch. He kept right on winging northward, as though he were the only ship in the sky.

The action sent Dusty's heart down into his boots. He cursed softly. Damn Washington! The pilot ahead had heard, and knew that he was safe from serious attack!

With a savage gesture, Dusty booted the Silver Flash over on a wing and sliced down sidewise.

"We'll see if you can take it!" he grunted aloud, and yanked the stick back into his stomach.

Tuned and rigged to a hair, the Silver Flash responded immediately. It tore straight at the attack ship. But in the last second the Yank tapped rudder and moved the stick over and back.

Up went the Silver Flash, its wheels seeming to virtually roll across the glossy surface of the top wing of the attack plane.

Cutting out and around, Dusty looked back. A hard smile tugged at the corners of his mouth.

"So?" he roared. "Just a little too close for you, eh, yellow belly? Well, have some more, and a few slugs just to make you feel even worse!"

Thumbs jammed against the trigger trips, he cut back in at the other plane. A dozen feet from it, he jabbed the trips and sent steel whining across the narrow space.

But as the last bullet ripped out, he suddenly released the trips and pulled the Silver Flash off to one side. Sucking on his oxygen tube, he leaned forward and stared through the glass cowling at the other plane. A moment later he was sure. There was more than one man in that other ship.

Faintly he could see a black-uniformed figure crouched forward in the cowled pilot's cockpit. But it was what he saw in the gunner's cockpit that held his eyes.

It was the figure of a man in ordinary civilian clothes. He couldn't see the man's face, because a black sack completely covered the head. But from the way the hooded figure sat rigid, he guessed that the man was bound hand and foot.

For a few moments Dusty circled the ship, trying to get closer for a better view of the strange human cargo in the gunner's cockpit. But as Browning guns suddenly clattered death at him, he kicked the Silver Flash into the clear.

That had been close! Dummy that he was, he'd forgotten about the plane being fitted with guns, and its pilot had waited for a neat broadside blast. But for a fool's luck, and his armor-plated cockpit, he might be now slamming down into the waters of the Atlantic.

But he only took a second out to curse his stupidity. Then he wheeled around and thundered down on the other ship. This time he meant business with capital letters, and for two nerve-shredding seconds he actually dragged his wing-tip across the top wing of the other plane.

At least it was nerve-shredding for the Black pilot. For with a violent movement, the attack ship cut down for a lower altitude.

But altitude didn't make any difference to Dusty. He could handle the Silver Flash at three feet or three million feet. With eyes blazing, he fanned the mystery pilot lower and lower.

Orders had been not to shoot it down. Okay, then, he wouldn't. But Washington had said nothing about wing-tickling the plane until it fell into the swells of the Atlantic. And that's just what Dusty intended to do.

The sight of the hooded figure in the rear cockpit had flooded him with an eerie premonition. Somehow he knew that the hooded figure was not a Black.

AND THEN, suddenly, the other pilot did a strange thing. Totally ignoring the Yank's wild strafing, he ruddered around straight out to sea.

For a moment Dusty was caught flat-footed. He gaped wide-eyed. And then with a muttered curse he sent the Silver Flash thundering after it.

But even as Dusty closed in, the other pilot pulled a second cockeyed maneuver. The attack plane spun around in a complete reverse and came charging, both guns blazing.

It wasn't even close this time. Hands, feet and brain working in perfect coordination, Dusty slipped into the clear, cut around and charged in like a man-made meteor gone berserk.

The charge was never completed, however. With plenty of air space still between the two ships, Dusty suddenly let out a wild roar and pulled the Silver Flash right up on its tail.

And well he did, for a split second later a blast of hell sliced the section of air where he'd been, and a dozen Black "Dart" monoplanes flashed down out of the sun.

Boiling with rage for having dropped into the trap, Dusty booted the Silver Flash over on wing, and slid crazily across the sky.

A jet-black monoplane got in front of his guns. He jabbed the trigger trips and the monoplane became so much junk slithering down to a final end in the watery folds of the North Atlantic. No more than five seconds later another monoplane joined the first.

But the loss of two of their kin only served to fire the efforts of the remainder. Like winged demons straight from hell, they fell upon Dusty.

A thousand singing deaths twanged off the armored sides of the cockpit, and "snicked" across the glass cowling. For the next few moments it was all he could do to keep Death's clutching fingers from grabbing him fast.

Skill will tell eventually, however, and no Black pilot was a man-to-man match for that wild flying Yank. With a wing-screaming maneuver he finally broke through the death ring and went careening off into the clear. But the joy that was his was fleeting. For the attack ship was thundering northwest toward land far down on the horizon.

Dusty Ayres had lost his quarry.

In another five or ten minutes he would have slapped that attack ship down into the water, and ridden herd on it while he called for a coast patrol boat to rush out and pick up its occupants. But now—

He left the thought unfinished and grabbed the transmitter tube.

"Emergency… emergency! All planes in or near Area P-Seven. AT-8 ship rescued by Black squadron. It's now headed for P-Seven. For Gads sake head it off. Will try to keep Black patrol from riding as escort. Send M.R. check-back!"

Breathlessly he waited for the "message received" signal to crackle in his earphones. But none came. Turning on full transmitter power he repeated the message three times, and then waited again.

Suddenly a voice spoke—a harsh, rasping voice—and Dusty's heart seemed to explode inside of him. On land, on the sea, or in the air, he'd know that voice anywhere.

"Sorry, Captain Ayres," it said, "but you are just wasting your breath. We have our transformers set at maximum power, and while you remain east of us, I doubt that any of your words will get through."

Truth hit Dusty like a bolt of lightning from the blue. That was right. He was east of the Black patrol and so long as they ran their set transformers wide open, his words would be just a jumble of sound to anyone trying to listen in.

Hell, yes, he could hear the transformer hum in his own earphones. True, the Blacks couldn't communicate with their own base until they let up on "blanketing" the air. But they didn't need to. Their job was to kill all knowledge of the AT-8's position.

But the thing that made his eyes go agate, and his thumbs slide up to the trigger trips, was the voice that had spoken to him. The voice of the Black Hawk!

A faint tinge of regret raced through him. So, the Black Hawk hadn't died after all? Somehow he'd been able to save himself from that sea of fire at Duluth? Or—or was perhaps this man a new Black Hawk?

When he had first met the Black Hawk face to face there had been five others with the man, identical in stature, facial expression and dress. At the time the Hawk had explained that they were his doubles—Blacks who represented themselves as him whenever he deemed it necessary.

Of course, that partly explained the reason for the Hawk's title, the Man With a Thousand Lives. His death had been reported in Europe an unlimited number of times. But always the Hawk seemed to come back from the grave.

Had the man who died at Duluth been one of his doubles? Or was he really the Black Hawk, and was this a new one—a new one to keep up Black Invader morale?

The answer to both questions was No! The voice, its pitch

and its tone, told him that the Black Hawk still lived, that he was in one of those monoplanes now closing in for the kill.

That settled in his mind, he flung the Silver Flash around in a dime turn.

"Okay!" he roared wildly. "We will make it definite this time!"

Crazy words, fired by a crazy idea. Hell, which of those ships piling down held the Black Hawk? They were all Darts, of the same type. All jet-black, and with no markings to distinguish one from the other. But what the hell did he care which ship held the Hawk? They were all Hawks to him, and to get the right one he'd blast them all down!

ALL HOPE of catching the AT-8 plane was gone now. A quick glance across the sky at the dot, fast losing itself in oblivion, was proof enough. He could only pray that some of the other Yank ships might cross its path before it swung inland.

But even that hope was practically out of the realm of possibilities. He'd been able to overtake the AT-8 because of the speed of the Silver Flash. But right now the AT-8 was off the Nova Scotia coast, many miles clear of the nearest Yank air base in Maine.

Okay, but it was going to cost these Blacks plenty. And with a bit of luck on his side, he was going to cost them their vulture-faced leader, the Black Hawk.

With that one thought burning in his brain, he hurled the Silver Flash across the sky, straight into the bullet-spitting mouths of the Blacks' guns.

It was a crazy maneuver, yet one that was perfect at certain times, and this was one of those times. The Blacks, possibly

suspecting a retreat, had bunched together so as to concentrate their fire.

But now a man eagle had whipped around and was slashing straight at them, and they were caught flat-footed. Desperately they tried to break up their diving wedge formation and scatter.

And all of them except one succeeded. That pilot died before he could even move the stick. One second he was the killer, and the next he was the killed.

"One!" howled Dusty. "Come on, you rats. Come on and take your medicine!"

But, strangely enough, the rats suddenly became possessed with a different idea. Instead of trying to trap the American ship in circle fire, every Black monoplane cut down and back, like a flash of black light.

"No you don't!" bellowed the Yank, and raked the nearest ship from cowled nose to tail wheel.

It dropped like a lump of lead, and lost itself in the Atlantic far below. But its going brought little consolation to Dusty. Mad clear through, he had but one desire, to battle them all, and slap them down one by one.

But he wasn't given the chance. What was left of the Black patrol had suddenly raced into full retreat, and was now tearing air toward the northwest.

For a moment Dusty didn't understand, and then with a gulp he realized that he'd unconsciously switched off his wave-length set. With quick motion he snapped it on, and almost immediately the answer for the retreat came to him.

It didn't come in the form of so many spoken words in his earphones. What he heard was furious dot-dashing in code. He couldn't make out a single letter. But the very fact that he couldn't, was his answer.

The dot-dashing was not coming from an American land station, because the regular International signals were not being used. A Black station was sending out words over the air in the secret Black Invader code that had been developed during the siege of Europe. Its very formation, which was a secret to the rest of the world, made it possible for Black operators to send out messages faster than any other code system known.

Not knowing the code, Dusty could only guess that the Blacks were being recalled to their base.

For a moment the Yank toyed with the idea of roaring after them. He could overtake them and continue the scrap. His was the faster ship. He'd proved that beyond a doubt ten days ago at Duluth.

Yet, on the other hand, the retreat of the Blacks had allowed sane reasoning to seep back into his head.

He'd been trapped once; why run the risk of being perhaps trapped again?

To the northwest, in the direction the Blacks were headed, was Canadian ground occupied by the Black Invaders. Chances were that he'd eventually fly into a sky full of Black ships. That was what these lads were probably trying to make him do, lure him into the claws of a Black fleet.

The thought brought a grunt to his lips.

"Yeah, you may be fair, Dusty, old kid. But you're no miracle-man. You'd get a bellyful of steel before you could flip a wing down. Take it on the chin, kid. You flopped your act. You caught the AT-8 and lost it again. So—"

He shrugged and left the rest unfinished. The best thing to do was to report the flop to Washington H.Q.

But as he reached out his hand to the wave-length dial knob, he suddenly let it drop back in his lap. A voice was barking in the earphones.

"Captain Ayres… Captain Ayres! Washington H.Q. speaking. Send a check-back. We've been trying to get you for twenty minutes. Captain Ayres, can you hear me? Can you hear me?"

He leaned forward to the transmitter tube.

"Captain Ayres to Washington. M.R… M.R. Go ahead, Washington!"

"Report progress, Captain Ayres!" ordered the voice in the earphones.

Dusty swallowed hard, started to report his failure when the voice suddenly cut him off.

"Never mind, Captain Ayres! H.Q. orders you to report here at once. Cease all activity and report here at once. This is an emergency H.Q. order. Signing off."

The earphones clicked and went dead. A low humming told Dusty that Washington H.Q. was trying to locate some other station, and was blotting out his own wave-length.

He leaned back against the seat rest and scowled at the dash panel.

"Damn it," he muttered aloud, "they didn't give me a chance to report anything. Just busted in with new orders."

CHAPTER 3
DEVIL'S RANSOM

FIVE MILES north of Washington field he signaled the field dispatch officer, received an "all clear" reply, and then stuck the nose down through a thin cloud layer.

Ten minutes later he sat down on the field and taxied up to the hangar line. Legging out, he started to give ship orders to a mechanic corporal, but broke off in the middle.

A big, shaggy-browed man in a staff general's uniform was walking rapidly toward him. Dusty's face lighted up with delight.

"Didn't expect you to meet me, sir," he said, snapping a salute.

The other, who was General Horner, Chief of Intelligence, but better known as X-34, nodded shortly and took Dusty's arm.

"Don't talk, Ayres," he boomed. "Come along. I've a car over here."

The pilot followed him over to a staff car, and climbed in. The general took the wheel, pressed the shift button, and sent the car spinning down the tarmac.

Once they were clear of the hangar line, he half turned his head.

"Give me all the details, Ayres," he said.

In crisp tones the pilot told his story from beginning to end.

"If those Blacks hadn't shown up, sir," he finished, "I think I would have forced it into the water, to float around until a patrol boat picked it up. But—"

"Not your fault," grunted the other. "Sure you didn't hit either of them?"

"Damn sure, sir! But I could have done it easy enough. I'd like to ask some questions about that, General. I—"

He stopped short as X-34 shook his head abruptly.

"No questions yet, Ayres. You'll hear about it presently, from somebody else."

Dusty relaxed. Out of the corner of his eye he studied the rugged features of General Horner.

The man's face was strained and drawn, and the near corner of his mouth twitched spasmodically. A blind man could tell that he was worried close to the breaking point.

Realization brought a little thump to Dusty's heart. General Horner occupied a top position on his admiration list. During the first few days of the war, X-34 had been his immediate superior. Tough and blunt to almost a fault, the general had proved himself a real man in the end. But there was another bond, other than personal acquaintanceship, that attracted Dusty to him. And that was an Intelligence Department operator known as Agent 10.

His meeting with Agent 10 had been a strange one. It had come to pass while he, Dusty, was a prisoner in the hands of the Black Hawk. Together they had smashed a Black Invader maneuver at Duluth that was crippling the entire communications system throughout the United States.

And then they had parted, Dusty to go his way on the American side of the lines, and Agent 10 to go his dangerous course as a Black soldier behind the Invaders' lines.

But later, Dusty had heard the truth from General Horner's lips—that Agent 10 was Horner's son.

He opened his lips to speak, to ask Horner if he had heard from his son. But suddenly he sat bolt upright in amazement.

General Horner had swung the car off Pennsylvania Avenue and was guiding it between wide gates and up a gravel drive to a building known to every man, woman and child in the United States. It was the executive mansion of the President—the White House.

An officer of the Presidential Guard of Honor saluted smartly as Horner braked to a gentle stop. A couple of Secret Service men closed in, gave them a searching look, then nodded and stepped back.

With a jerk of his hand to follow, Horner stepped out and hard-heeled through the glass doors that swung wide at his approach. Just inside the door a uniformed attendant stopped them. General Horner fixed him with a steely eye.

"Please tell the President that General Horner and Captain Ayres have arrived."

"This way, sir," the attendant said mechanically, motioning to the right. "The President is expecting you."

With that, the attendant walked across the Rotunda floor and knocked on a huge oak-paneled door. Waiting a second or two, he pushed open the door, and stepped to one side. Giving Dusty a side nod, General Horner stepped through into the adjoining room. Blood tingling through his veins, Dusty followed.

THE PRESIDENT, seated behind a massive desk at one

end of the richly furnished room, returned their salute with a nod and a smile.

"Be seated, gentlemen," he said in his soft yet penetrating voice. As they removed their service hats and seated themselves, he looked to Dusty.

"Before we turn to other matters, Captain Ayres, I want to compliment you for your gallant service during the Duluth invasion. Neither words, nor the special decoration which Congress will shortly bestow on you, can in any manner express the full gratitude of your countrymen."

Dusty bowed stiffly.

"I thank you, sir," he somehow got out. "But I am sure that it was no more than any other loyal United States citizen would have done had he been afforded the same opportunity."

The President smiled. Then slowly the smile faded and a look of grave worry and concern seeped into his lean face. His deep blue eyes flashed to General Horner.

"You have spoken to Captain Ayres, General?"

Horner shook his head.

"No, Mr. President. I believe the story should come from your lips alone."

For a moment there was absolute silence. Then the President spoke again.

"Captain Ayres," he began, "two days after the retreat from Duluth, the commander-in-chief of the Black forces communicated with this government suggesting a proposition whereby permanent peace throughout the world might be restored. The United States was given ten days in which to agree to arbitration. Naturally, we would never agree to any form of arbitration with the Black forces. But, we decided to take advantage of the ten day period and build up a defense against the Blacks' position in Canada. Also—"

The President paused and cast a sidelong glance at General Horner.

"Also," he repeated, "we had hopes of checkmating the Blacks once and for all. Through General Horner's men we found the supposed location of Fire-Eyes' headquarters in Canada. Every man in the Intelligence Service was put to work—the idea being to capture the entire Black high command staff. We failed in the attempt. Our agents had not found the real H.Q."

Again silence settled over the room. Dusty had the feeling that something would blow up with a terrific roar at any second. Rigid, he glanced first at the President, then at General Horner. Both were staring fixedly into space.

And then the President turned to him again.

"The attempt, and failure," he said, "told Fire-Eyes of our intentions regarding his peace proposition. And before we realized it, he beat us at our own game."

The President reached into a drawer, took out a sheet of paper, and handed it to Dusty. The pilot stared at the pen-scrawled words.

To the President:

You have until four o'clock to agree to my arbitration terms. If you do not, your son will be placed in a loaded radio-controlled bomber and flown into the Washington Capitol Building.

Fire-Eyes

Dusty read it over five times.

"Your son," he gasped.

"My son, Charles," finished the president in a low voice, "was kidnapped this morning shortly after eight o'clock, and flown to Black territory in Canada. That was the AT-8 plane that you had orders to force down."

For a moment Dusty's brain spun crazily. The figure with the hood over his head, in the rear cockpit of the AT-8 crate, had been the President's son?

"You mean, sir, he was kidnapped right here in Washington?"

The Chief Executive nodded sadly.

"I mean just that, Captain. Charles was on his way to visit one of his young friends in Georgetown. Halfway there a car with Maryland plates pushed his car off the road. The Secret Service man who was driving was shot and killed instantly. Charles was overpowered and driven off in the other car. Fifteen minutes later he was in the air, a prisoner, and on his way north."

"But that AT-8 plane!" Dusty exclaimed as the other paused. "It's attached to the Washington field. Where is the pilot? How was it possible to steal his plane?"

The President looked at Horner.

"You found out about that, General," he said.

The Intelligence Chief grunted.

"All part of their plan, Ayres," he rumbled. "That AT-8 belongs to Lieutenant Stafford. According to the field flight log he was up making a test. Somehow, by a short-wave field set I guess, they managed to signal him to land at the old abandoned Army field near Georgetown. When he did, they shot him, and took the ship. He lived long enough to get to the nearest phone. He died at the phone trying to tell his field commander what had happened. That note you just read was dropped over the Georgetown infantry depot. The plane was not seen again until you met it."

DUSTY GROANED as memory of meeting that plane flashed back to him. Without thinking he blurted out the words that rose to his lips.

"God, why didn't you say who was in the plane? If I'd only known that, I'd—I'd still be trying, instead of returning here."

The President smiled faintly at the explosion of youthful declarations.

"You had your orders, and you obeyed them as a good soldier should," he said. "Charles' name was not mentioned in that emergency order because we wish to keep the thing secret. And, I had you ordered back here, because—because it would have been useless for you to continue the search. You see, when that return order was sent out to you, we knew that Charles had been landed in Black territory."

"You knew?" Dusty blinked.

"Yes, we knew," was the positive reply. "The Blacks got in touch with us on our official wave-length, and we heard Charles' voice tell us that he was a prisoner behind the Black lines. He started to shout something else, but he was stopped."

The President's voice faltered, and broke. His hands resting on the desk top doubled into hard fists, and his face went ashen. To Dusty it was like a knife twisting in his heart to witness the terrific struggle the leader of his country was waging against complete breakdown.

This wasn't war! The President's son was but an eleven-year-old lad, who had been more or less under a specialist's care since birth, when his mother had died. He wasn't a soldier facing death on the battlefield, taking his chances with thousands of others. He was just a youngster, and an invalid at that!

But to the Black Invaders, that boy was a powerful weapon. With him they could strike at the President of the United States. Blood is blood, and those devils knew it.

"After my son had spoken to me, Captain," went on the President, "Fire-Eyes himself came on the air. He wanted to make a bargain with me. He wanted to exchange a life for a life. He agreed to return my son, if I surrendered you, Captain Ayres!"

Dusty could only stare for a moment, then he got to his feet and saluted.

"I hope you agreed, sir," he said. "I am ready."

"Sit down, Captain! I haven't finished. Here, look at this!"

The President slid a thick square of paper across the desk top. It was a printed announcement.

PEOPLE OF AMERICA

The world wants peace! We do not wish to war on your women and children.

We have tried to reach terms with your government, but we were refused. Your leader values personal life of his kin above country. His son is in our hands. We offer his safe return to your President for peace.

What will his answer be?

Will he sacrifice his son's life for war?

Will he sacrifice the lives of others for his son's life?

We wait for his final answer tomorrow. What will it be, People of America?

The Army At Your Gates

"That's just how clever they are," General Horner said, pointing a thick finger at the last line. "The answer tomorrow, according to that, but we know that Fire-Eyes is supposed to get his answer at four o'clock this afternoon!"

Dusty nodded. That point had not missed him. He glanced at the President.

"When and where did you get this, sir?"

It was Horner who answered.

"One of my agents picked it up on the street, about an hour ago," he said. "Since then fifty others have phoned in telling me that they found them. Right now, I'll bet my commission, these cards are scattered throughout every city in the country."

The pilot stared at the card again. He felt stumped. Give him an enemy ship with flame-spitting guns, and he'd ask for nothing better than the chance to smack it down. But this kind of war—this stabbing in the back in the dark—

He jerked up his head quickly, met the President's eyes.

"I suggest, sir," he said, "that you agree to the exchange. That will at least get your son back, and I'm ready to take my chances with them. I've done it before, and I can do it again. In fact," he added slowly, "I would rather relish meeting the Black Hawk again."

The President smiled faintly.

"I admire your courage, Captain," he said. "But even to save my own son, I couldn't issue an order like that."

"Orders be hanged, sir! I'm volunteering for this job, and I demand that I be accepted!"

He stopped short, leaned over and rapped his knuckles on the printed card.

"Be damned to that sort of thing, and what the people may think. The main thing is to get your son back. Don't worry about me. I always come back. I insist that you agree to the exchange when you speak to Fire-Eyes at four o'clock!"

THE PRESIDENT lowered his eyes, and sat silently scowling at the desk top. Dusty turned to Horner and was surprised to see a smile fading from the Intelligence Chiefs lips.

But before he could speak, the jangle of the desk phone echoed through the room.

The President's eyes flickered to it, and for a split second he seemed to hesitate. Then he picked up the instrument.

"General Horner? Just a moment. For you, General."

The Chief of Intelligence barked into the mouthpiece, then snapped his lips shut and listened.

"Good work, Peters!" he snapped in reply. "Watch him. I'll be right over. Bye!"

Jumping to his feet, he slapped the instrument back in its cradle, and leaned over the desk toward the President.

"Something to work on, sir!" he exclaimed. "That was Peters, of my department. It seems that Lieutenant Stafford helped us more than we thought. He wounded one of the bunch that got your son. The wounded man tried to get first-aid in Georgetown. One of my radio-patrol operators happened to see him, got suspicious and tailed him to a house we've been watching for some time. There was a gun fight, but my operator got his man. They're holding him at the Department now. If you'll excuse me, sir, I'll rush over."

The President nodded.

"Certainly, General. Let me know how you make out."

"Yes, sir. Come along, Ayres. Please excuse us both, sir."

Heels together, they clicked off smart salutes to their Commander-in-Chief, received the dismissal nod, and about-faced and left the room.

Dusty started for the front door. The attendant who had admitted them began to open it, but General Horner stopped him.

"Never mind, Barton. Come this way, Ayres! It's quicker."

The pilot followed the Intelligence Chief to a small elevator at the left rear of the Rotunda. Horner jabbed the button and the car shot downward.

As they stepped out onto a long platform Dusty gasped in surprise. They were standing on the platform of a narrow-gauge electric subway station.

"Didn't know about this, eh?" the big man grunted. "Installed almost four years ago. Connects every government building in the District. Damned good thing, too. Saves all kinds of time. Come on, in you get!"

As though the man's words were some sort of a magic signal, a small car slid out of the dimly lighted tube hole at the right, and came to a gentle stop in the center of the platform.

It was a low, streamlined car with seats for ten passengers. A sliding door clicked open and Horner virtually shoved Dusty inside. He reached his hand toward a button panel. Beside each button was the name of a government building. The general's finger jabbed the button beside the name "War Department."

The next thing Dusty realized, an unseen force was pressing him back against the seat, and the glow of dim lights was flickering past the long, narrow, reinforced glass window of the car.

For a dizzy instant he had the impression that he was inside a torpedo that was being shot out of its compressed air tube into bottomless waters. And then the flying instinct within him took charge of his scattered senses, and he relaxed.

"A kick for even our leading speed pilot, eh?"

Dusty turned his head and looked into the grinning face of Horner.

"We usually warn first-time passengers about the quick start," smiled the Intelligence Chief. "But I was just wondering how your nerves were."

The pilot frowned.

As he started to figure out that remark, there came a soft hiss of escaping air; the car shot alongside a narrow platform and came to a gentle stop.

"Out we go!" announced Horner.

Dusty followed him out onto the platform toward an elevator door. He absently noted a uniformed guard pacing slowly up and down the platform at the far end.

He gave him but a glance, started to walk through the opening doors of the elevator, but jerked to a dead stop as the rapid fire blast of an automatic crashed against his eardrums. At the same instant there was a thudding sound. General Horner staggered backward against the elevator doorjamb.

CHAPTER 4
BLACK MURDER

FOR AN infinitesimal flash of time, Dusty stood stock-still. Then his right hand whipped down and up, and his body half turned. The service automatic in his right hand belched flame and sound.

A horrible scream merged in with the echo. The uniformed guard at the far end of the platform spun around twice and then toppled over. A gun still clutched in his fingers smacked against the cement.

"Good shooting, Ayres," puffed Horner's voice. "But hell, man, you've killed him!"

Dusty whirled to see the Intelligence Chief slowly getting to his feet.

"You hurt bad, sir?" he asked.

"Hurt—hell! Just winded! Been wearing this bulletproof vest for weeks. That's one thing the rats didn't know. Let's take a look at him."

Horner puffed down the platform to the crumpled figure.

When the pilot caught up with him he was toeing the body over.

It was an ordinary face; that is, apart from the stamp of death upon it. But it had no distinguishing features. Its owner could be, or rather, could have been, a native of a dozen different countries. But he was a member of the Devil's legions now. There was no doubt about that. All eight of Dusty's shots had caved in his chest.

"Yes, neat shooting, Ayres!" grunted Horner. "But a damned shame, nevertheless! It's a human impossibility to make a dead man talk."

"Sorry, sir!" Dusty grated. "But I didn't know about your vest, either!"

Horner gripped his arm and pressed hard.

"Easy, lad," he soothed. "I apologize. I went off half-cocked. But I haven't been able to grab a Black agent alive, yet. It's funny, but somehow death always beats me to it. I—"

He suddenly cut himself off, and scowled down at the dead man.

"Hum-m-m!" he mused aloud. "I haven't used this for four or five days. Now, I wonder—"

Spinning around, Horner raced for the elevator.

On the fifty-sixth floor of the building the car came to a stop, and the doors automatically rolled open.

Out ducked Horner, without so much as a glance at Dusty. It was as though the Intelligence Chief had forgotten his existence entirely. But the pilot stuck to his heels, followed him into his private office.

...THE SERVICE AUTOMATIC IN HIS HAND BELCHED FLAME AND SOUND.

Going over to the inter-department call-set on the desk, General Horner rapped down a contact arm switch and bent over the transmitter.

"Collins! This is Horner. Grab the White House Rotunda attendant and bring him here at once! And stick a couple of your best men on the President. Get it? Stick 'em on no matter what he says. Yes, I'll take all the responsibility. Now, hop to it!"

Flipping up the switch, the general dropped into his chair and glared at Dusty.

"By God," he boomed, "here's where I get one of them alive!"

Horner's hand shot out to the switch panel again.

"Hicks?" he barked. "Send Peters in with that man at once!"

They both stiffened as the reply came through the speaker.

"Peters, sir? He hasn't been in for an hour, sir. He went over to the SS Files office, I believe. Did you—?"

"Come in here, Hicks."

Horner's booming voice echoed and reechoed about the four walls of the room.

"Y-y-yes sir!" gasped out the speaker horn.

Hardly had the Intelligence Chief snapped off the switch than the side door opened and a thin, white-faced staff orderly slipped inside.

"You—you want me, sir?" he gulped fearfully.

The general leaned forward, eyes narrowed.

"Ten minutes ago, Hicks," he snapped, "Peters told me that he was holding a man here for questioning—a Black agent. Do you mean Peters hasn't been here for an hour?"

The staff orderly's head bobbed up and down like a marionette's.

"That's right, sir!" he exclaimed. "I'm positive! I've been holding some code-grams for him, sir. And I've been waiting in his office all the time. I think you'll find him at the SS Files, sir."

The general started to speak, then changed his mind.

"All right, Hicks," he grunted. "That's all. Get out."

As the orderly popped out again Horner bent over the inter-department call-set.

"Secret Service Files!" he grunted. Then, "SS? Horner. Is Peters there? Is, eh? Send him to me at once, and tell him to bring the dossier on every man in the White House. That's right. The SS record on every one of them!"

As Horner snapped off the connection a heavy silence settled down over the room. Dusty cleared his throat.

"Mind telling me, sir?" he ventured.

The other shot him a keen look.

"Can't you guess it?" he asked.

"Partly, sir. The Rotunda orderly was the only one who saw us take the subcar, and, of course, he probably signaled ahead to that fake guard. But why did he leave me in the clear? I was nearer to the guard than you were."

The other drummed on the table for several moments.

"He wanted to make sure that I would go out of the picture," he said eventually. "Damn it, I was a fool not to have suspected such an attempt. They've tried it often enough!"

AT THAT moment the door opened and a heavy-set, middle-aged man entered the office. A bulging brief case dangled from the fingers of one hand. With the other hand he flicked off his hat and half saluted.

"Here you are, sir," he said, dropping the brief case on top of the desk. "Something popping?"

Horner ignored the question, snapped open the case and started thumbing through the stack of file folders it contained. He pulled one out, read it through carefully.

When he placed it back on the desk and raised his head, there was a savage gleam in his eyes.

Did you call me at the White House a quarter of an hour ago, Peters?" he suddenly shot out.

"Why, no sir, I didn't call you."

The general glanced at Dusty.

"Ten to one that sub guard is imitating voices in hell now," he grunted. Then, as though struck with sudden inspiration, he jerked his eyes back to Peters' face.

"Go down to the sub platform, Peters. There's a dead man down there. Get his prints and compare them with any you find on the signal phone booth. And, listen, check on the central call recorder, too. Get going!"

As the junior Intelligence man went out the door, he paused long enough to stare hard at two burly men escorting a man in uniform. Then he stepped aside to let them through, and dashed on his way.

The uniformed man was the attendant in the White House Rotunda. Dusty felt a sudden touch of pity for him.

The hatchet face had lost its blank expression. The eyes were wide and watery, and every drop of color had seeped out of the spotted skin. Here was fear and terror, if the pilot had never seen either before.

But there was no pity in General Horner's eyes. If anything, there was a look of berserk desire to commit murder with his bare hands.

"Sit down in that chair!" he rasped out.

The operators released their hold and the attendant practically fell into the chair. He sat crouched sidewise, watery eyes fixed on the floor.

"Your name John Barton?" cracked out Horner's voice.

The attendant jerked a half nod.

"Yes, sir," he husked.

Horner went over to him, hooked the fingers of his right hand under the man's chin and propped it up.

"All right, John Barton!" he snapped. "Where is Fire-Eyes' H.Q.?"

The watery eyes blinked rapidly.

"For God's sake, sir!" he choked. "What are you talking about? I don't understand you."

General Horner snorted.

"You might as well talk," he said in a low, penetrating voice. "It will go easier with you. In fact, I'll promise a prison term instead of a firing squad."

He broke off sharply, waited a moment, eyes riveted on the upturned face, then spoke again.

"Now tell me. What happened to the real John Barton? What

did you and your rat friends do to him? Kill him and destroy the body? Come now—speak!"

The attendants features twisted and jumped about all over his face. Twice he started to speak, but couldn't seem to get the words out. Then finally they came out in a torrent of sound.

"For the love of God, sir, what are you saying? I swear to you I am John Barton. I'm not a Black I'm an American, I tell you. And I love my country. I object to this treatment. I demand that you—"

"Shut up!"

The command was like a whip-lash across the attendant's face. His thin lips clicked shut, and his face blanched even more.

Horner let go of the man's chin, and stood straddle-legged, eyeing him coldly. It was a good three minutes before the Intelligence Chief spoke again. And when he did, there was a soft persuasive tone in his voice.

"Why be a fool, man?" he asked gently. "I've caught you, and you know it. We'll forget about the real John Barton. The poor devil's dead. Whether you killed him or not, I don't know. But it was arranged for you to take his place. How long have you been acting the part—six months?"

The attendant shivered, shook his head.

"I tell you, I am John Barton!" he said thickly. "I've been in the White House service for five years! The personnel records will prove it!"

"And all you have to tell me," went on General Horner, as though the other had not spoken, "is the exact location of the H.Q. of Fire-Eyes. I give you my word—not a word will be mentioned as to where we got the information. Come now, my man, why face a firing squad when you can save your life?"

THE UTTER dejection and misery on the attendant's face flooded Dusty with a sense of anger against General Horner. Damn it, the Intelligence Chief was using third-degree methods with no foundation but circumstantial suspicion to base his actions on. Hell, the attendant was in a blue funk of fear, and didn't know what he was saying.

But it was obvious that X-34 did not share Dusty's thoughts, for he suddenly grabbed the attendant in one huge paw and virtually lifted him clear of the chairs.

"Answer me, you little rat!" he roared. "Answer me, or I'll stick you up against the firing wall within the hour!"

The man's teeth were chattering too much for words to come out. With a snort of rage, Horner dropped him and he fell back onto the chair gasping for breath.

Hands locked behind him, brows furrowed, the general started pacing slowly up and down the room. Twice he glanced at Dusty, read the frank disapproval in the pilot's eyes, and grunted. The third time he stopped, and fixed Dusty with a cold look.

"You can wait in the other office, if you want to, Captain," he said tartly. "This is the dirty side of war, you know."

"I'll stick, sir," he said quietly. "But justice usually demands proof, doesn't it?"

The other started a hot retort, then cut it off short, as though he suddenly remembered that his battle was with the White House attendant and not with Dusty Ayres.

Lips pressed tight, he walked over to the desk picked up the file folder and spread it out on his two hands. Then he turned and faced the attendant.

"So you swear that you are the White House attendant known as John Barton, eh?" he asked.

The other nodded violently.

"Yes, sir!" he gulped. "That's right. I swear it!"

"Well, then," said Horner softly, "tell us about that accident when you were fourteen."

The answer came back immediately.

"I was in a motor smash-up and broke both legs. It was in the papers. I still have a clipping about it."

"Anything else?"

"No-o-o, sir. Not that I remember."

Horner smiled, and walked close.

"Your superiors did a good job when they checked back on John Barton's history," he said. "But, like many other things, nine times out often there is always a slip-up somewhere along the line. One little insignificant thing that they overlook. The police have caught a million crooks that way—just the way I've caught you!"

To Dusty's surprise the attendant's head jerked up and his eyes blazed into Horner's.

"You haven't caught me!" he cried. "You haven't, because I am John Barton! I don't care if you are a general, I'll report this, you see if I don't. I know my rights!"

Horner cursed softly, shot out his free hand, grabbed the man by the hair and jerked his head back so hard that he yelped with pain.

Holding him in a savage grip, Horner tapped the right under part of the man's jaw with a corner of the file holder.

"In that motor crash!" he snapped. "The real John Barton broke both of his legs, and got a sliver of glass in his jaw! One year later it was taken out and the scar has been there ever since! There's no scar on your jaw! Now, will you answer my question?"

"There was a scar!" choked the other. "But it wore away two years ago!"

Rage, berserk rage, flooded the general's face and for an instant it looked as though he were going to crash his sledge-hammer fist into the spotted, yellowish upturned face.

Perhaps he would have, had not the door opened at that instant, and Peters stepped inside. The staff operator glanced at his chief and nodded.

"You were right, sir," he said. "The prints checked perfectly. And the call recorder shows that there was a call from the White House rotunda to the sub-platform at two-twelve."

The general nodded, and let his eyes flicker across Dusty's face, then faced the attendant.

"Your last chance," he said evenly. "Where is the exact H.Q. of Fire-Eyes? Remember, you have my promise. It will be prison instead of a firing squad. You're trapped, so you'd better save your own hide and speak."

The attendant sat still as death for a moment. Then slowly he raised his hands to his head, as though trying to shut out all sound so that he could think.

He pulled his hands, claw-like, down over his face and started chewing on his nails, his eyes darting crazy like from side to side. A second later his whole body trembled and his hands dropped onto his lap.

"Speak up!" bellowed Horner, red faced. "Tell us where—"

He cut off the rest with a savage curse, and bent close to the attendant. The man's face had taken on an ashen gray hue, and his eyes had become dull and glassy.

"Damn it to hell!" Horner's voice snapped bitterly. "Licked again!"

As he spoke he lifted the man's right hand, turned it palm up and stared at it for a moment. Then with a long sigh he let the hand drop, and turned toward his desk.

Peters' voice crashed against the silence.

"My God, chief! He's dead!"

Horner turned, the corners of his mouth pulled down, and nodded.

"Of course he's dead!" he growled. "See that crusted paste under the fingernail of the little finger? That's where he kept the poison. The rat feared death, all right, but he feared Fire-Eyes more. Hell!"

TURNING BACK to the desk again, General Horner went over to it and sat down heavily and gazed unwinking at the polished top. Presently he looked up at Peters.

"Take it out of here," he grunted, with a side nod at the dead man. "You two help Peters, then make your reports for the official record."

A minute later only Horner and Dusty were left in the room. Horner turned to him with leveled eyes.

"You still feel the same way now, Ayres?" he asked quietly.

"My error, sir," Dusty answered quickly. "I guess I'd make a bum Intelligence operator. I thought he was innocent. Guess I'll keep right on sticking to the flying end. At least I'll know who my enemy is."

The other smiled sadly.

"That's what you think," he said. "But as time goes on you'll find out that modern war doesn't mean armed men and machines lined up against each other on the field of battle. There is no Front, as there used to be years ago. No matter how far behind the battle line you may be, you are still on the battle front. And that is the secret of this new move of the Black Invaders—they are smashing into the heart of our country. Their weapons are not guns and shells, but intrigue and the ultimate cracking down of faith in government and enemy morale."

Dusty put forward the question that was foremost in his mind. "How about my suggestion, sir?"

Horner slanted a look at him, cleared his throat.

"Sure you want to, son?" he said slowly.

Dusty's voice crackled. "Of course I do! Give me the word to go—or I'm going without it!"

The general smiled broadly.

"The fire-eater lets off steam, eh?" he chuckled. Then went deadly serious. "Yes, the thing to do is to get the President's son back alive before Fire-Eyes can use him as an effective weapon of war. But I'm also thinking of you, lad."

Dusty grinned and shook his head.

"Then stop thinking about me, general," he said. "I'll hold up my end. You just arrange for the President to agree to the exchange, and leave the rest to me. Get word through to you—to Agent 10, that I'm coming over. Maybe he and I can team up again and beat them."

General Horner's face went suddenly gray and old.

"Agent 10 was killed during the raid on what we believed to be the Black H.Q.," he murmured. "I received that news by secret code from another agent, yesterday morning."

Stunned, Dusty leaned back weakly against the chair. To him the death of Agent 10 was a personal loss. A brave, gallant and fearless pal—dead. It couldn't be true. Agent 10 was too fine to be allowed to meet a spy's death hundreds of miles from his comrades in arms. Yet, he was dead; a brother agent had sent the sorrowful news through.

From a long way off, Dusty heard Horner's voice speaking again.

"Now, perhaps, you realize a little more fully my treatment of that White House attendant?"

Dusty didn't answer. There was nothing he could say. As a matter of fact, he was too ashamed of himself to try to say anything. How would he have treated a Black agent if his son had been only twenty four hours dead? God, he would have tossed duty into the discard and torn the man limb from limb.

"But that's a closed book, Ayres. And there still remains the job to be done. By clever work on the part of the Blacks the President's hands are tied. If his son dies in Black territory, they'll broadcast the story that other Americans died trying to rescue him on the President's orders. In other words, soldiers sacrificed to save the life of the President's son. If the President agrees to Fire-Eyes' terms they'll do the same thing. And lastly, if the President refuses to agree and his son is sent over here in a loaded, radio-controlled bomber, what else can we do but shoot it down?"

"No pilot would obey such an order!" broke in Dusty. "No American pilot would deliberately murder the son of his President!"

General Horner gestured significantly.

"Just the point," he said. "But either way, the result for the Blacks would be just the same. The President's son would die, and the Capitol building would be blown off the face of the map, while the Army, Navy and Air Force did nothing about it."

"But why talk of that angle?" cut in Dusty. "I'll go park with the Blacks, and the President's son will come home. We just want to be sure that they don't pull any tricks, and keep the boy. I suggest that the transfer be arranged so that you'll be sure to get him."

Horner nodded.

"Yes, I've been thinking about that ever since I had you ordered back here. I—"

"You had me ordered back?" began Dusty. "Why, the President—"

"Right," smiled the other. "I ordered you back, and not the President. Why? Because I knew damned well that you'd volunteer for this job. And it's his duty to say no, regardless of losing his own son. But I think different. So do you. That's because we're both soldiers. However, even I wouldn't order you to do it, lad. Huh, guess I knew I wouldn't have to. But I had to make sure, you see."

Still smiling, the Intelligence Chief got up, gripped Dusty's shoulder hard, and started toward the door.

"Wait for me, Ayres," he said over his shoulder. "I'm going to see the President and make him agree to the exchange. You'll find cigarettes in the box, there."

CHAPTER 5
BLACK LIGHTNING

FOR THE next half hour, or more, Dusty concentrated on smoking the general's cigarettes, and trying to figure his chances in the big event to come. Would Lady Luck stick with him through this new venture—or had she already tired of watching over his tough hide? But why worry? He wasn't dead yet—he'd escaped from the Blacks before, maybe he could do it again. And there was a bit of a kick in the realization that he made enough of an impression on those Black bums to make them want him so much.

With a shrug, he started to light the last cigarette in the box when the door popped open and a staff lieutenant stuck his head inside.

"Captain Ayres? General Horner's compliments, will you please go up to the radio-room on the roof, right away?"

Dusty nodded, stubbed out the cigarette. Three minutes later he was walking down the steel-walled corridor that led to the radio-signal control room on the roof of the War Department building.

Without bothering to knock, he stepped into the sound-proof room where almost two weeks ago he had heard the President refuse the impossible demands of Fire-Eyes, just before the Black attack on the United States.

That answer had been a declaration of war against the Black forces.

Memory of those dramatic moments returned as he once again saw the walls of laminated steel and copper. Here was the very heart of the nation. This room was the key point of the United States Government communication systems. By simply throwing a switch and turning a dial one could talk with any point in the country or world in a matter of split seconds.

But what held Dusty's attention the most were the people in the room. At the far end sat Major Jordon, chief signal officer of the department. And at his side were the President and General Horner.

They acknowledged Ayres' entrance with a nod, and turned back to the instrument panel in front of them.

"I think he's trying to get us now, sir," Major Jordon said tensely. "He's working on wave-length six-zero-four."

"You are sure there is no leakage, major?" asked the President.

"Positive, sir," was the prompt reply. "If he talks on six-zero-four no other station can possibly cut in. The signal vibrations are too high. Ah—in a minute, sir! Hear that oscillation? He's tuning power up!"

A high-keyed humming sound filled the room. Higher and

higher it went until it was no longer possible for the human ear to detect the sound.

And then, seconds later, the panel speaker crackled. A moment or two more and the crackling merged together and became spoken words.

"Calling U.S. Official on six-zero-four—calling U.S. Official on six-zero-four!"

The voice was harsh, rasping, and Dusty stiffened as he realized the identity of its owner. Once before he had heard that same voice, and in this very room.

The other time Fire-Eyes had spoken over the Telerad system, and they had all seen his black-mantled figure transposed on the Telerad screen. But this time only his voice was coming to them.

Hardly realizing what he was doing, Dusty glanced at his wrist watch, and absently noted that the hands showed exactly four o'clock.

And then he forgot about the time as he heard Major Jordan's clear voice.

"Signals received on six-zero-four. Signals received on six-zero-four. Go ahead."

Giving a dial a hair turn, the signal officer motioned the President closer to the transmitter. Dusty held his breath.

And once again the voice of Fire-Eyes, command in chief of the Black Invaders, grated against his eardrums.

"Mr. President! It is now four o'clock. What is your answer to my last message? Do you agree to my terms, or shall I be forced to return your son to you the other way?"

Tingling silence followed the words. The President's body went rigid. General Horner's face paled slightly. He put out his hand quickly and pressed the President's arm.

And then the Chief Executive spoke, slowly and clearly.

"Your original peace terms are refused, sir. But I agree to your last proposition—that of exchanging prisoners. I suggest that the exchange take place tonight and in the following manner.

"For the period of one hour, beginning at midnight, the area on the northwestern border of the State of Maine, known as J-Twenty-seven, will be regarded as a neutral zone. A unit of our searchlights will flood the southern part of the zone. And a unit of your searchlights will flood the northern part.

"At twelve sharp you will release your prisoner and permit him to walk south through the neutral zone. At the same time our Captain Ayres will walk north toward your lines. Captain Ayres will be instructed not to speak to your prisoner when they meet. And I request that you instruct your prisoner accordingly.

"As the zone will be lighted, both sides will know when the exchange has been completed. And when it has, the neutrality of the area will cease at once. Is the plan acceptable?"

Ears strained, Dusty could have sworn he heard a faint chuckle coming over the air. But if it was a chuckle it was drowned out almost immediately by Fire-Eyes' harsh voice.

"It is acceptable, Mr. President. But I warn you that guns will be trained on our prisoner, and any attempt to rescue Captain Ayres will be met with absolute resistance."

BEFORE THE President could reply to the threat, the panel

speaker clicked and the sound wave went dead. For a long moment the Chief Executive sat motionless, staring at the panel.

Then he got up and walked quickly over to Dusty, and laid a hand on the pilot's shoulder.

"My boy," he began, "I have no right to ask you to do this thing. If there were only—"

His voice faltered. Dusty stiffened to attention.

"I have only one desire, sir," he said, "to serve my country, to the very best of my ability."

The fingers on his shoulder tightened, and the President opened his lips to speak again.

"Pardon, sir, we haven't much time. And I wish to talk with Captain Ayres."

The President turned at the sound of General Horner's voice. He nodded slowly.

"Very well, general," he said, "the whole thing is entirely in your hands. I only—", he glanced sidewise at Dusty, "I only hope and pray that you meet with success. I could never forgive you for failure, general. You know that?"

The Intelligence Chief saluted stiffly.

"I understand perfectly, sir. I would never forgive myself, either!" And then to Dusty. "Come along, Ayres."

Dusty felt the President's eyes fixed on him, and then the next second he was hard-heeling out of the radio control room and down the steel-walled corridor in the wake of General Horner. Down they shot in the elevator to the street level, and then out the front entrance of the building to a waiting staff car.

Horner motioned Dusty in and turned to the uniformed driver, who was already reaching out a finger toward the shift button on the dash.

"Military field, sergeant, and fast!" Horner snapped. "Don't stop for anything."

"Right, sir!"

No sooner had the general piled in back than the car slid away from the curb and hummed down Pennsylvania Avenue. In a fog of perplexity, Dusty leaned toward his superior.

"The military field, sir?"

The other cut him off with a gesture.

"You'll see presently!" he bit off.

With a sigh Dusty leaned back against the cushions. Ten minutes later the car rolled to a stop on the tarmac of the military field, and Horner jumped out. Dusty was out in a flash and dropped into step with his superior.

As they reached the end hangar, a sergeant ran up and saluted.

"All set, sir, as you ordered."

Dusty's eyes followed the man's nod. There was a small cabin plane on the line. Its prop was clicking over slowly, and a couple of mechanics stood waiting at the wing-tips. His own ship, the Silver Flash, was also on the line, but there were no mechanics near it.

He frowned and glanced questioningly at General Horner. A faint smile, was tugging at the corners of the general's mouth.

"I'm considering using that cabin plane as an official executive ship, Ayres," he said. "As you are the best pilot we have, I want you to test it out, and give me your frank opinion. Come along. I'll ride with you."

Raging anger shook Dusty for a moment. My God, what next? With his career as a war pilot practically signed, sealed and delivered, damned if Horner wasn't using up his last moments of freedom by handing him a test flight job!

"Right, sir!" he nodded with a savage effort at self-control. "Let's go!"

Avoiding the other's eyes he walked over to the plane and legged in. A test flight, eh? Okay, he'd give General Horner the ride of his lifetime—a little sky jaunt he'd remember for a long time to come.

Holding back long enough to allow the general to get in and seat himself, Dusty nodded the mechanics clear, booted the brake release, and whammed home the throttle. The ship practically leaped into the air from a standing start. Grimly pleased that Horner had gone spilling back on his neck, Dusty heeled the wing over, scraped up some of the drome grass and then pulled the ship up, prop-on for Heaven.

"Ayres, damn you—stop it!"

Dusty leveled off a bit, turned in the seat and glanced innocently at the upset general.

"Sorry, sir," he said politely. "I was just testing the speed of the takeoff. She handles very nicely, sir. A pretty good ship—so far."

Face red and chest heaving, General Horner settled himself

back on the seat and glared at his pilot. Then slowly the anger faded from his eyes, and he smiled slightly.

"All right, son," he said quietly. "I know just how you feel. But I had to do it this way. The thing's too damned dangerous to take any chances at all. Let's see, is that radio off, absolutely?"

Dusty glanced at the dash set, and noted that the dial knob was at zero.

"Yes, sir," he said. "And now, if you'll pardon me, what the hell's the idea of this?"

"Simply a precautionary measure, Ayres," replied the other. "With Black agents practically popping out of my hair, there are damned few places where I dare talk. Up here, however, is the one safe place. And now, Ayres, I'm going to tell you about the arrangements for tonight."

WITH A sigh of relief, Dusty started swinging the trim little cabin ship around in a series of lazy circles, and waited. He didn't have to wait long.

"The President has given me carte blanche permission to carry out a plan I have in mind. Incidentally, the President does not know about it. He only knows that I have one. To insure the utmost secrecy I have not told anyone, as yet. But as you are the key man, I am going to tell you. Bluntly, there will be no exchange of prisoners tonight. I suppose you are familiar with the Maine J-Twenty-seven area the President mentioned?"

Dusty nodded.

"Yes, sir. That's just east of Frontier Lake on the Quebec border."

"Correct. It runs diagonally across the line. It's a nature-made pass between two rows of pine-studded hills, about a mile long and not over a hundred yards wide at the widest part. Now, listen carefully.

"At ordinary walking speed it should take you about twenty minutes to go from one end of that valley to the other. That would place you on the Black side at twenty minutes past twelve. At quarter past twelve you should be within a quarter of a mile of their lines. And—it will be at twelve-fifteen that we spring our little surprise on Fire-Eyes."

The general paused, deliberately.

"And the surprise, sir?" Dusty encouraged.

"Just this," the words shot back. "Lieutenant Banks, the best Gyro pilot in our service, will pick you up. And in the meantime we will open fire on the Blacks and over your escape. The President's son will be near enough to our lines for us to rush out and grab him, before the Blacks can do anything.

"And after that—the armed forces of Uncle Sam will go into action in earnest. Once Banks pulls you clear of the ground it will be the signal for the American advance into Canada to begin. And, by God, well give those blasted Blacks plenty to think about this time!"

There was a ring of savage determination in Horner's voice as he spoke, but it found no corresponding echo in Dusty. The plan left the pilot cold and unimpressed. Sure, it was great on paper. But how about the Blacks knocking Banks' Gyro into eternity before he came down for a vertical landing?

He put the question to Horner.

"Who said anything about Banks landing?" the general

... DUSTY THREW IT INTO A VICIOUS WHIP-SPIN.

snorted. "That's the big point. Banks will hover over that spot at low altitude, and at exactly twelve-fifteen, he will come down a little lower and drop a pick-up ladder. Once you grab it, he will go up. As additional protection for you, while you're swinging on the ladder, the beams of our searchlights will be thrown straight at the Blacks. You've done pick-up work before, haven't you?"

Dusty nodded. He had, many times. It was a part of troop contact training, and with modern equipment it was very simple.

A Gyro hovered over a given spot of ground, where the contact pilot had theoretically crashed. By pulling a release lever the Gyro pilot could open a trap in the bottom of his fuselage and a double rope ladder shot earthward. The "crashed" pilot simply grasped it and climbed upward to the Gyro; which was in the meantime getting vertical altitude.

Yeah, it was a good emergency maneuver, all right, but with the eyes of half a million Blacks on him every second, well—

Dusty finished the thought with a shrug.

"I reckon I can do it, sir," he said quietly.

The general stared thoughtfully ahead for a moment.

"It's our only chance, Ayres," he said after a while. "I wish to God I could take an active part, instead of gambling with the lives of other men. But there's no other way out. I've gone over every angle of the whole thing.

"If we can but trip Fire-Eyes up this time, it will mean a lot more than you could possibly realize. You've got to believe me in that, Ayres. It will be the snapping of the key strands of a propaganda web that may eventually spell defeat and ruination for us all."

Though the importance of propaganda didn't impress the sky eagle much, Dusty realized that General Horner was in deadly earnest. The Intelligence Chiefs face was drawn, and in ten seconds he seemed to have aged ten years.

"Don't worry about me, sir," Dusty said quietly, nosing the ship up through a cloud layer. I'll get away in that Gyro, all right. Just tell Banks to be sure and let her rip full out, once I grab the ropes. I—"

He never finished, for at that instant Horner shouted and pointed ahead and up. Even before Dusty could snap his eyes in that direction the staccato yammer of aerial machine-gun fire crackled against his eardrums.

HANDS AND feet working like twin flashes of lightning, Dusty hurled the ship on wingtip, cut around in a dime turn, and then reversed. A faint tremor rippled through the ship and his war-tuned brain told him they had been hit.

"Hang on!" he yelled at Horner. "I'm going to spin out!"

Action and words became as one. The little cabin ship seemed to groan in protest as Dusty threw it into a vicious whip-spin. But somehow the wings stayed on and the plane corkscrewed earthward like a falling rocket.

The engine roared and pounded on its bearers, and Dusty had to use every ounce of his strength to hold the inherently stable craft in its wild maneuver. All the time the savage snarl of machine guns followed them down through the air.

Though he'd only gotten a glance at the jet-black wings which cut down through the air, Dusty knew instinctively that the little cabin job was no match for the mysterious attacker. To try and run for it was out of the question. Better to whip back and settle it with guns instead of speed.

A kick on the rudder and a tap on the stick brought the plane out of its mad spin and round on wing-tip. In the second the sudden maneuver afforded Dusty, he got a good look at the other plane. Saw clearly its black biplane wings, built into the top and bottom of the barrel-shaped fuselage, and the stubby tail with its four-strand radio mast.

Though he'd never seen the type before, Dusty guessed that it was a flying radio laboratory. The kind of plane used for controlling radio bombers.

Fast as the ordinary run of ships, its main advantage was its altitude possibilities. Heaven was the ceiling—its cabin being sealed and fitted with temperature and air rectifiers and equalizers.

For a moment Dusty stared at the ship, fascinated by the originality of its design. Then with a curse he slid his thumbs up to the trigger trips. It was a cold meat shot.

But, a split second later his heart went cold. His clawing thumbs found no trigger trips. The cowled nose of the cabin plane contained only gun brackets, but no guns.

Then the radio ship cut around and out of the cold meat area. And it continued right on cutting around, too. Seconds later its twin guns again spat flame. Dusty whirled and spun his ship about, missing death a thousand different times.

Hugging the seat pad, eyes staring dead ahead, General

Horner crouched like a man turned to stone. But Dusty didn't even give him a glance. There was no time to wonder how his passenger was taking it.

The Black radio ship was cutting corner after corner, and it was only a matter of time before its pilot would pin the cabin ship against the nearest cloud.

"Like hell you will! Like hell you will!"

Not hearing his own voice ringing in his ears, Dusty yelled the words over and over again, and kept right on, whipping his little craft away from the steel-jacketed messengers of death which zipped after him. Then, suddenly, a plan of escape came to him.

In one continuous movement Dusty shot out his free hand, snapped on the radio, spun the wave-length dial to the Washington military field reading, and scooped up the transmitter tube.

"Military Twenty-four!" he roared. "Military Twenty-four. Have Black radio patrol ship cornered right above you at twenty-three thousand. Send up fighting planes at once. Will try and force ship down to their level. Hurry—emergency!"

As the last word tore off his lips, Dusty swung in close to the radio ship, cut up above it and then started straight down. A second later he grinned. The idea had worked! The radio plane had picked up his ground call, and its pilot wasn't taking any chances of an uneven scrap.

With a sudden burst of speed, the Black ship slammed out from under Dusty's diving plane and streaked heavenward.

Hunched over the stick, Dusty watched it disappear in the upper air.

There was only one crate that could climb faster than that radio ship, and that was the Silver Flash. But the Silver Flash was twenty thousand feet below. With a faint feeling of regret he "lost" the radio ship and checked his own climb by leveling off.

"Okay, sir?" he grinned at the white-faced Horner. "I guess he doesn't want to stick around."

The Intelligence Chief made three attempts to speak, and succeeded on the last.

"God, son!" he got out. "That was close—too damned close. Thank God, your brain worked when mine stopped. Go on down, and land, Ayres."

"I don't like it!" Horner went on. "Somebody signaled that ship that I was going up. And how the devil did it get here, anyway—right here over Washington?"

"I can answer the last, sir," Dusty said. And then told him of the ceiling possibilities of that type of ship.

"He could very easily slide over at top ceiling," he finished. "Our observation patrols wouldn't be that high, and therefore would never see him."

"But why over Washington?" grunted the other. "That's what I can't understand."

Dusty steepened the glide, and helped things along with a bit of engine goosing. As he swung in to land he half turned to the general.

"Maybe he was taking a look-see in case he has to maneuver the Black bomber."

"Exactly!" grunted the general, as the wheels touched turf and the cabin plane rolled gently forward. "It's either that—or something else."

WITH THOUGHTFUL eyes he watched Dusty taxi up to the hangar line and skillfully one-wheel braked the ship around, nose to the field. Then, suddenly, he spoke.

"It's either that Fire-Eyes does not intend to give up the President's son, or that he's got his signals crossed with his subordinates. In either case—"

At that moment a red-faced field major came running up. He jerked open the cabin door and glared at Dusty.

"Say, Ayres, what the devil's the idea of playing tricks on us!" he roared. "One of my flights has just radioed down that there isn't the sign of a ship up there."

"There was, Major!" Horner snapped at him. "But it's gone!"

The field officer noticed him for the first time and gulped.

"You, sir? I—I'm sorry, I didn't realize. But there was a ship, sir?"

"There was!" repeated Horner as he legged out. Then, suddenly, he pointed toward the tail of the plane. "See them, Major, those bullet holes? We didn't put them there. And by the way, Major, there are no guns on this plane. How do you account for that?"

The field officer's eyes raced to the cowled nose, and his face paled. For a moment he couldn't get the words off his lips.

"Why—I don't understand, sir!" he stammered. "I—I tested

this ship this morning, and I'll swear it was fitted with guns, two rapid Brownings. Why, every ship here is supposed—"

"But this one wasn't!" Horner cracked down on him. "I'll wait in your office, Major. Get the maintenance mechanic on this plane and bring him to me, at once."

Without waiting for the other's salute, Horner walked to the field office. Dropping his big frame into the nearest chair, he scowled savagely at nothing in particular.

Dusty, who had followed, lighted a cigarette and idly glanced at the flight chart fastened to the wall.

Several minutes passed before the door opened and the field major burst inside.

"He's gone, sir!" he gasped. "Hasn't been seen for hours. And I've just found out that he wasn't on the field personnel records. No listing of his name—Palmer."

The Intelligence Chief nodded slowly. A few moments later he jerked up his head.

"Let me see your radio-log for the last ten days," he ordered.

"Yes, sir," bobbed the other, and darted over to his desk.

HE CAME back almost immediately with a clip file of radio-station reports. Horner thumbed through them slowly. Presently he stiffened and grunted aloud.

"Very, very clever—damn their hides!"

"You found something, sir?" gasped the field major.

"I found that a man named Palmer has been relieving the radio operator on duty during the breakfast hour, for the last five days," said Horner.

The major sighed with relief.

"That can't mean anything, sir," he said. "As you know, this field station is dead every morning between eight o'clock and nine. It's inspection time, and the infantry station at Alexandria handles all messages. The operator on duty here is allowed to let someone spell him while he goes to the mess for breakfast. It's a system we've been following for years!"

Horner slowly got to his feet, and his big face clouded over like a thunder storm.

"Unfortunately, Major!" he boomed, "in this case it happens to be a damned poor system! A very important event took place at eight forty-five this morning. And shortly after that I phoned this field to put my plane in readiness for flight on a moment's notice.

"Both those bits of information were undoubtedly communicated to a Black radio plane high over this field—communicated on a supposedly dead station by a Black agent known by the name of Palmer.

"I'm requesting you to make arrangements for two men from my department to be taken on as mechanics here at the field, just in case some friends of Palmer's try to carry on from where he left off."

"Yes, sir!" gulped the major, his face as white as a sheet. "I'm sorry, sir. I—it's my responsibility—I'm—"

"Just keep your eyes open for everything, Major," Horner cut him off gently. "I'm not blaming you in particular. Keep on the alert every second. Come along, Ayres."

Getting into the staff car, they started back to Washington.

"So that's how Lieutenant Stafford was signaled down at the

old Army field near Georgetown, eh?" he murmured. "It wasn't a short-wave field set, as you thought?"

Horner nodded gloomily.

"Correct! Another one of the thousand times I've been guessing wrong, lately. When we reach town, I'll drop you at my office. Jordon will come down and keep you company. If I'm not there by ten o'clock you and Jordon go to the field, get a plane and fly to the southern end of J-Twenty-six and wait for me. If I don't turn up by twelve—well, the whole thing will be in your hands from then on. Got it all?"

"Yes, sir," Dusty nodded. "But where are you headed? And why wouldn't you show up?"

The other frowned.

"I'm going to chat with a certain pilot—get it? And if I don't show up, it will simply mean that a man's luck doesn't hold out forever!"

CHAPTER 6
VALLEY OF DEATH

FOR THE hundredth time Dusty glanced at his wrist watch. The time was exactly nine forty-eight. He lighted a cigarette and looked at Major Jordon lounging comfortably in the chair opposite him. For almost four hours now, they had been keeping each other company.

Not knowing just how much the radio control room officer knew, Dusty's conversation had been guarded and strained. Both had discussed the war from every conceivable angle, yet obviously avoiding the development of the day, and the events to come.

Somehow Dusty had the feeling that Jordon knew almost as much as he did, and several times questions trembled on his lips. But he always bit them back and said nothing.

And now, with only twelve minutes to go to the deadline, General Horner had not put in an appearance, or communicated with them in any way.

"I wish to hell he'd show up!" the pilot grumbled.

Major Jordon studied his cigarette.

"You never can tell about his actions," he said quietly. "I've seen him pop up lots of times at the very last second."

Dusty leaned forward.

"You know that you are to fly north with me at ten?"

The other smiled almost paternally.

"Naturally, Captain. And put your mind at rest. You've been like a hen trying to hide the fact that she's got an egg in the nest. You're forgetting that I was there when the President spoke to Fire-Eyes."

Dusty said nothing. He simply nodded. At ten sharp he looked at Jordon and stood up.

"Zero hour, sir. I guess we'd better get going."

The major nodded silently and reached for his service cap.

Fifteen minutes later they were on the military field tarmac watching a group of mechanics give a final tune-up to a sleek-looking, center-winged, observation ship. A moment later the corporal in charge came forward and saluted.

"All set, sir," he said to Dusty.

The pilot nodded, started to step through the cabin door to the pilot-observer compartment, then suddenly stepped back and motioned Jordon to get in.

"Be right with you, sir," he said.

Before the senior officer could ask any questions Dusty spun around and ran into the center hangar and over to his parked Silver Flash. Had anyone been watching him at that moment, they would undoubtedly have thought he had gone crazy. But then, they couldn't possibly have understood the feeling of that sky eagle for his plane.

A half smile on his lips, he ran his hand along the glossy wing surface.

"I'll be back, old girl!" he murmured, "we're not busting up this team yet! Not by a damn sight!"

And then he turned quickly away and raced back to the observation ship. Without a word he climbed in, un-braked the wheels and palmed the throttle forward.

The movement of the ship was the signal to the officer in the take-off tower. Immediately, sunken lights in the field turned the runway bright as day. Slow on the start, the plane rolled fifty yards or more, then pulled itself free and curved up into the night.

ONCE IT was clear, the field lights winked out, and Dusty sensed an eerie feeling that seemed to cling about him like a damp shroud. Countless times had he roared up into the limitless expanses of air, but never once with the spine-tingling sensation he had at the moment.

He felt as though he had left behind everything he knew

and understood, forever. And that he was traveling toward a strange and terrible world from which no human had ever returned.

With a savage effort he shrugged the sensation off and glanced sidewise at Major Jordon. If the radio officer was experiencing the same emotion, it was not betrayed on his face.

Features almost cold and impassive, he was lounging back against the seat, idly watching ground lights whip past far below.

The man's attitude gave Dusty a sense of peacefulness. Leveling off just beneath a cloud layer, he set the ship on a bee-line compass course for his ultimate objective far to the north. That done with, he cut in the engine muffler and relaxed.

Seconds whipped past and became minutes. Eventually the minutes became an hour; ticked on toward the second hour. Neither of the men in the plane spoke.

And then, suddenly, as they winged across the Massachusetts-New Hampshire line, there took place in the heavens a nocturnal phenomenon so strange and eerie that it brought both men up stiff in their seats.

At first the thing seemed like a square mile of dotted light silhouetted against the bottom part of the cloud layer. But a few seconds later they were able to see that the light dots were in rows and curves—that they formed letters against the cloud layer, as though it were a giant projection screen against which a picture was being projected.

But this was not a picture. The square mile projection screen in the sky contained only letters—that formed words!

"My God, look!" Jordon gasped. "Look what it says!"

There was no need for Jordon to have spoken. Dusty was already reading the gigantic sign.

AMERICANS

YOUR PRESIDENT DOES NOT WANT PEACE.
HE HAS AGREED TO GIVE THE LIFE
OF YOUR GREATEST AIRMAN FOR THE RETURN
OF HIS SON.
WE OFFERED PEACE BUT HIS
ANSWER WAS WAR.
WHO WILL BE SACRIFICED NEXT?

From away off Dusty faintly heard his own roaring voice.

"That's a lie—a damned lie, you devils!"

He turned to Jordon.

"How the hell can they do that? Throw that sign into the sky, I mean."

Jordon's face went hard.

"Simple!" he grated. "And damn them, they beat us to it! I've been working on the same idea for a year. Got it all set to work, too!"

"Got what all set to work?" Dusty snapped, as the other hesitated.

Major Jordon gestured.

"We call it a searchlight gun," he said. "The idea of it is just what you see up there now—to throw words against the clouds, far behind the enemy's lines."

"Then that thing's coming from Black territory?"

"Right!" the other nodded. "The projector is five hundred miles from here, if it's a mile. But the idea isn't new. It was tried out years ago.

"It's simply a question of sufficient candlepower filtered through a lens-plate upon which the message is punched out. From the main lens, the so-called gun, telescopes outward. The telescopic projector is fitted with specially designed light absorbers that cut down the side reflection, so that the light-beams coming through the holes don't spread out and merge with each other. But, damn them, they've beaten us to it, again!"

Dusty said nothing. He was staring narrow-eyed at the sky sign. It had been east of them when they first saw it, but now it had moved across the heavens and was far to the west. His eyes went agate as he thought of the millions of Americans who must be reading that sign—reading it, and drawing their own conclusions.

What were they thinking now? Was this lie taking root in their upset minds? Or was—?

The Yank speed ace smothered the rest with a curse.

Swinging a bit eastward, he throttled and let the ship slide gently earthward. In a glance he checked his course instruments with the roller map on the dash, then leaned forward and stared hard at the ground ahead. A minute later, and he had his position pin-pointed exactly. Twenty minutes more on this course and he'd be there.

Fifteen of the twenty minutes slid into history and then he suddenly saw the faint red, glowing landing T a bit ahead and far below. Without saying anything he touched Jordon's arm and pointed. The radio officer looked down for a few seconds, then nodded.

"That's it all right. Five lights for the cross bar, and nine for the vertical. I guess we'll find the general waiting for us."
BUT JORDON'S guess was wrong. Five minutes later Dusty had slipped in to a perfect landing on a dime-sized field and was listening to a very excited infantry officer.

"But the general informed me by wire that he'd be in your ship!" the man was exclaiming. "For, God knows why, I've got a mobile searchlight unit here, two machine gun companies, and a company of infantry.

"What the hell's it all about? Why in blazes did they make this place a neutral zone? Is H.Q. crazy? On the other side there's a hundred thousand Black troops. There'd be hell to pay, if they decided to come at us. Our main line has swung back on both flanks."

Dusty started to speak, then shut his mouth and said nothing. The infantry officer gazed at him helplessly, then switched his eyes to Jordon. The radio officer glanced at his watch and shrugged.

"We've got fifteen minutes yet," he said slowly. "I guess we'd better wait and see if General Horner shows up."

Though the tone was casual, Dusty caught the undercurrent of worry. The infantry captain must have sensed it, too, for he suddenly leaned forward.

"You think maybe he won't, Major?"
Jordon shrugged again.

"Let's wait," he repeated. Then looking directly at Dusty, "If he doesn't show up, we'll take our orders from you, Ayres."

Dusty nodded grimly. As though expecting to see the Intelligence Chief suddenly pop into existence, he gazed across the small landing field—and saw nothing but the night ground shadows. Though he tried not to do it, he looked to the north, to the entrance of the narrow valley which ran across the Canadian line into Black territory.

Ten minutes more and that now-dark valley would be flooded with light from end to end, and he would start his gamble with death. Ten minutes more—nine—eight—

He turned to the infantry captain.

"Your mobile light unit," he said, "it's trained on that valley?"

"Yes," the other nodded. "Orders are to flood it at twelve sharp, and hold it until further orders."

"And the infantry and machine gunners?" Dusty asked.

The other pulled down the corners of his mouth.

"That's what I want to know!" he snapped. "What in hell does Horner plan to pull off a daylight raid with a handful of men and guns? Why we'd be cut down before we got five feet!"

The pilot didn't answer. He simply shrugged and stared skyward. Presently, Major Jordon spoke.

"Four minutes to go, Ayres! I guess you'd better let us in on the rest of Horner's plan. I guess he isn't coming."

The words were like machine-gun bursts in Dusty's ears. He sucked in his breath, then let it out with a long sigh.

"All right," he said quietly. "Now, listen carefully. This is the plan of action."

In swift, to-the-point sentences, he told them all what Horner told him.

When he finished, the infantry officer whistled softly, and stared at him.

"Lord!" he gasped. "The President's son? I'd heard rumors, but I didn't think—"

"Save it!" Jordon cut in sharply. "Snappy, now! You take charge of the searchlight unit. I'll handle the gunners, and the rescue party. Get going, you haven't a second to lose!"

With a nod and a flicked salute, the infantryman darted off across the field. Jordon turned to Dusty, put out his hand.

"A million in luck!" he said in a husky voice. "Well, let's start up there, now. And listen, lad, I'll blast them away from you single-handed, if I have to!"

"Thanks," grunted Dusty.

He was hardly conscious of his own voice, for at that moment cold, clammy fingers were clutching at his heart. Was Banks up there waiting for him?

"This is far enough. Only a minute to go, now."

Jordon's voice broke in on Dusty's thoughts. With a start he realized that they were at the southern end of the valley.

A movement off to the right jerked his eyes that way. Dimly he made out the platform and huge globe of a mobile searchlight. Figures were swarming about it.

And then from behind him came the dull sound of clanking metal. He knew without turning that the machine gunners and rescue party were moving up into position. Unable to hold back the temptation he raised his eyes upward—and saw nothing but dark starless sky.

S–s–s–s–s–sop!

A tiny flare arced upward off to the left, and split seconds later, four shafts of brilliant light sprang into life. They turned the night-darkened valley into day. Almost at the same instant four more beams of light slanted down from the northern end of the gorge about a mile away.

"Good luck and God bless you!"

Jordon's voice echoing in his ears, Dusty slipped into the valley of man-made light, and walked northward. Save for his feet striking the earth, all about him was as silent as a tomb. Straining his eyes forward, he saw an empty valley, flanked on both sides by towering pine-spotted cliffs.

At the end of two hundred yards, he glanced down at his watch. It was 12:05.

Forcing himself to refrain from even so much as glancing upward, he kept right on swinging up the valley.

And then suddenly he saw it—the dim figure of a youngster. The figure was approaching from the left, head down and shoulders hunched. For one berserk second Dusty had the impulse to dash over, scoop up the small youth in his arms, and make a wild dash for the American side. But memory of Fire-Eyes' words checked him—"Our guns will be trained on the prisoner!"

Steeling himself, Dusty swerved to the right, and walked on past the hunch-shouldered figure, head up and eyes straight

A SPLIT SECOND LATER HE WAS HURLING HIS BODY FORWARD...

ahead. A second later he eased out a sigh of relief. That part of the play was finished.

From now on he was the only actor left on the stage. Jordon and the machine gunners would take care of the President's son. He glanced at his watch again.

"12:11!"

Forward, up the valley of light he continued, each step a step nearer the unknown.

And then the hands of his watch showed exactly 12:15. Directly ahead, less than a quarter of a mile away, were the Black lines. He could tell from the angle of the floodlights just where they were.

His footsteps lagged, stopped altogether. Then he stiffened as a thumping sound came to his ears.

A split second later he was hurling his body forward at a double rope pick-up ladder which hung dangling down out of nowhere!

A HUMAN torpedo charging through a sea of light. An iron eagle diving at the ladder of life. That's what that crazy Yank looked like as he shot himself through the air.

Every nerve sprung, every muscle taut, his body arched outward, and his clawing fingers clutched again, and hung on. Momentum carried the lower part of his body forward, and his feet hooked in the rope steps.

For a second he paused, fighting for breath. He couldn't see a thing, for all about was clear, white dazzling light. Instinctively he realized that the infantry officer was training his searchlight beams on the Blacks. And Jordon was doing his stuff with the machine gunners, too. The air was crackling with the staccato sound of rapid fire. Then he felt himself rising. Good old Banks! The Gyro pilot was taking him up, clear of the raging hell below.

Bracing himself, he started to climb the pickup ladder. Would he never get clear of that sea of light? The Blacks must be able to see him now—at any second they'd open fire, and blast him right off the ladder. Yet, as the seconds dragged by, not a single shot came from the enemy side of the valley.

And then suddenly, every bit of light fused out, and the American's rapid fire died away to an echo. Swinging slowly upward, Dusty clung to his aerial perch. He turned his head and stared downward. All he saw was the thin beam of a flashlight moving here and there. All was deathly still.

What had happened? Horner said that his clearing the ground would be a signal for a gigantic Yank offensive against the Black Invaders? Well, where was it?

His arms and legs ached from the tenseness of his muscles. He relaxed a bit, and started to climb again. The main thing right now was to get up into the Gyro, and then to get Banks to set him down behind the American lines. Then he could find out what had gone wrong.

Checking the swing of the ladder as much as he could, Dusty climbed upward. Eventually, he was able to hear the faint swish of the Gyro's blades. And when he threw back his head and stared above he was just able to see the dark blur that was the craft. Fifteen feet more to go—ten—five!

With a grunt of relief, he hooked a hand over the grasp rail at the edge of the fuselage trap. Gripping it with his other hand he kicked his feet free, and slowly pulled his body into the dimly-lighted cabin.

Fumbling for the clampholds of the pick-up ladder, he unsnapped them. As the ladder whipped down into oblivion, he slammed the trap shut and got to his feet. The next instant, the tired grin on his lips froze; his eyes narrowed into grim slits.

For there, standing spraddle-legged at the end of the cabin, gas-gun in hand, was the Black Hawk!

"GREETINGS, CAPTAIN Ayres. I've been hoping that we'd meet again soon."

The cold, rasping voice snapped in Dusty's ears. He stepped forward, one hand streaking to his holstered gun.

"Stop!"

The command was like a pistol shot. Dusty stopped dead in his tracks and his hand dropped to his side. He stood eyeing the Hawk coldly. The big hatchet-faced Black nodded his head and showed his fang-like teeth in a smirk.

"That is much better, Captain," he said. "After having gone to all this trouble, I should regret very much to be forced to kill you. And now, please hold that position!"

As the man spoke, he moved forward with lightning speed, whipped Dusty's automatic from its holster and struck it in his own tunic pocket. Steeling himself, the Yank looked past the Black to the front end of the Gyro. The figure at the controls was not Lieutenant Banks. It was a big man in the uniform of the Black Invaders.

The Hawk must have seen his look, and understood, for as he stepped back from Dusty he laughed.

"Surely you did not expect to see Lieutenant Banks, did you, captain?"

Dusty's eyes went agape. The Black Hawk gestured meaningly.

"When one fights a war, one does many things," he said. "Your friend, Lieutenant Banks, was not necessary to our plans—therefore, we got rid of him."

"But how did you find out?" Dusty snapped.

"We Blacks know a great deal, captain," the other smiled. "We have set a goal for ourselves, and nothing on the face of this earth is going to stop us from reaching it."

Dusty's lips straightened out into a thin line.

"You can't do it," he grated. "You're dealing with United States citizens now, Black Hawk."

"Exactly, Captain," replied the Black, dispassionately. "You Americans had your chance—the chance for an honorable peace. You refused. Now you are going to feel the consequences."

Dusty was seething with rage inside, but he forced himself to appear calm and unafraid.

"You're wrong again. I'm not the whole Yank army, I'm just one pilot, and I won't be missed. There's ten thousand others to take my place."

"Yes, yes," said the Hawk wearily. "I recall you saying the same thing once before when we had a little chat. But, you miss the point, my friend. We now have two important lives with which to threaten your President."

"Two lives," Dusty echoed thickly. "Why you dirty—" he checked himself. It would do no good to lose his temper now. "Then you didn't—"

"Didn't keep our part of the bargain?" the Black Hawk finished for him. "Certainly not, Captain. No more than you people kept your part. Did General Horner think we were stupid enough, not to see through your President's suggestion? We simply set about discovering the details of the plan, and made our own arrangements accordingly."

"But, hell!" snapped Dusty, "only three men knew!"

"Quite right," smiled the Black. "So we simply asked General Horner to tell us—and he did."

Dusty stood for a moment, like a man of stone, eyes riveted on the hatchet face before him.

"It's a lie!" he roared. "Why Horner is as white as they come. He wouldn't tell you a thing!"

Brows arched, the Black shrugged significantly.

"Then how else could we have found out, Captain?" he purred smoothly. "Think what you wish, but I assure you that General Horner told us everything, and with his own lips.

"Ah, wait a minute—do these words sound familiar? 'If I don't turn up by twelve—well, the whole thing will be in your hands from then on.' There, don't they sound familiar, Captain?"

As the voice smacked against his eardrums, Dusty felt that the bottom had dropped out of his world. Horner had spoken—

Horner had told the Blacks everything? But it just couldn't be true.

"I still don't believe you," he said between clenched teeth. "Horner would die before he'd tell you a damned thing."

"No, Captain," spoke up the Black Hawk. "General Horner did tell us everything—and he did not die. As a matter of fact, I imagine that right about now he is wondering what happened. Or, perhaps he is trying desperately to reach the nearest communication point."

"Where?" exclaimed Dusty.

The Hawk shrugged.

"I couldn't say, exactly. But, it's some place in your beautiful state of Maine. You see, General Horner is considerably more valuable to us alive, on his side of the lines. So, instead of killing him, we released him, so that he would return to Washington and be of further assistance to us."

WORDS—JUST WORDS that didn't make sense to Dusty, no matter which way he looked at them.

"General Horner wouldn't turn traitor," he said at last.

Loud laughter burst from the Hawk's lips, sent him rocking back on his heels.

"Turn traitor?" the man guffawed. "No, of course not. But, there are ways to make a man talk, you know, Captain."

Dusty bunched his fists unconsciously.

"Tortured him, eh?" he grated. "It would be your way!"

"Wrong again, Captain. Tell me, have you ever been present when a man was coming out from under the influence of an anesthetic?"

85

"Sure," nodded the pilot.

"Often times," smiled the Black Hawk, "a man in such a condition babbles out the thoughts uppermost in his mind. Do you understand me, now?"

When Dusty made no comment, he continued talking.

"Of course, we did not employ anything so crude or elemental as an anesthetic, in General Horner's case. We used something our chemical and gas bureau had developed. But the results were the same, in that the good general repeated aloud practically everything he had said for the last twenty-four hours.

"With that knowledge, our task was very simple. Naturally, our agents took care of your Lieutenant Banks. And here we are, Captain."

With a desire to stall for time, and perhaps catch the Hawk off his guard, Dusty spoke the question that was uppermost in his mind.

"But how did you catch General Horner?"

"Equally simple," purred the other, "Every move he made was known to us—has been for days. One or two over-zealous members of our forces tried to kill him. You recall an incident on the subway platform, and an attack by a radio plane of ours? Oh, don't look surprised, my friend. We Blacks naturally know every move our associates make. However, those over-zealous comrades will get their reward later, I assure you.

"But as I started to tell you, General Horner has not once been out of our sight. Our agents on the ground reported his movements by portable transmitters, to one of our stratosphere radio planes, which in turn reported them to our headquarters.

"Naturally, once we learned that he had had secret meetings with you, and with one Lieutenant Banks of a Gyro squadron, we suspected immediately that something important was being arranged. So we captured the general, treated him with what we like to call our Talk-Vapor, and learned all we wished to know."

The Black paused, smiled crookedly at Dusty.

"Perhaps, Captain," he leered, "you may wonder why I go to the trouble to tell you all this? It really is not just blowing about our achievement. On the contrary, it is merely to point out to your chief of Intelligence how futile it is to match his wits with ours. And as he is in total ignorance of what has taken place, I hope that you will tell him, yourself—should you meet him."

Dusty tensed just a bit at the last words. Cruel, pompous, and a windbag, the Hawk liked nothing better than to parade himself and his deeds before his prisoners. But there had been a peculiar undercurrent in the man's last remark. Should he meet him—would he meet Horner?

"Figuring on capturing him again?" he grinned scornfully.

"No," replied the Hawk easily. "Not unless an occasion warrants it. But—I see what you mean. Yes, Captain, I believe you will see the general again, very shortly. But the meeting will not be a happy one, at all."

With a smirk the Black Hawk turned his head and called something, in a strange language, to the pilot up ahead. And it was that split second of time upon which Dusty staked his life.

The Hawk must have suspected the thought in Dusty's brain, for even as the Yank crouched and flung himself across the cabin, the Hawk spun and jerked up his gas gun. But almost immediately he snapped the gun down, and crashed out his free fist.

The blow knocked Dusty's outstretched hands aside, skidded up his forearm, and smashed against his jaw. A world of colored lights exploded in his head, as he went reeling backward.

"Fool! You almost forced me to kill you that time. Now, I will make you quiet!"

The words made hissing sound in Dusty's ears as he struggled to his feet. And through the blur of dancing light a shadow whipped at him, then crashed down on the base of his skull. After that, he knew nothing but a world of ringing darkness.

CHAPTER 7
BLACK FORTRESS

WHEN DUSTY next opened his eyes, his first impression was that a jagged tooth buzzsaw was cutting through his brain. He groaned, put his fists to his temples and tried to press the pain away. It was then he realized that he was lying on his side on an iron cot, face to a stone wall.

Biting his lips against the pain of moving, he rolled over on his back and fixed glassy eyes on the ceiling. It was like heavy perfume. Or better still, like the interior of a hot-house.

He swung his legs off the cot and sat up. For a moment objects danced dizzily before his eyes. Then they ceased moving, and took on definite shapes. With a wild curse, he started to his feet, and stood staring toward the other side of the room.

Fifteen feet away was another cot and huddled upon it, eyes closed, his young face white and drawn, was the President's son!

Suddenly the whole picture was crystal clear in Dusty's brain. The Hawk had spoken the truth. The Blacks had not lived up to their end of the arrangement. That figure he'd passed in the J-Twenty-seven valley had been a substitute.

Hell, no wonder the lights had winked out, and the firing stopped so quickly. Jordon had discovered that the youth who trudged into their lines was not the President's son. And, no wonder the Blacks had not fired on him as the Gyro pulled him upward. There was no need for them to.

Hardly realizing what he was doing, the Yank leaped toward the prostrate lad. But before he had taken two steps, he crashed into something and went sprawling flat on the floor. As he raised himself to an upright position a moment later, he saw what had happened.

The room was divided into two rooms. And the wall between the two was of thick plate glass. Not realizing it was there, he had crashed blindly against it.

Getting up, Dusty went back to his cot and sat down. He stared for quite a while through the thick glass at the pale-faced youth. Was the youngster still alive? He looked so still lying there. He didn't even look as if he were breathing. And as for his face, it seemed drained of all blood.

Dusty went over to the glass partition and pounded his fist against it, called the lad's name. But the child remained still as death. Finally, still weak, Dusty stumbled back to the cot.

Face set grimly, he made a careful study of his new prison. He discovered nothing that gave him any hope.

Three sides of his room were stone. The fourth glass. A small door to his right was of steel construction. There were no windows in the room, but along the back wall, near the ceiling, was a single row of half-inch holes. The room in which the President's son lay was an exact duplicate of his own.

For the want of anything better to do, he got slowly to his feet and began pacing up and down the length of the room. The heavy perfume aroma was still in his nostrils, but it was not as strong as it had been when he first noticed it. In fact, it seemed to be disappearing rapidly.

On impulse, he stepped up on the cot, and reached up a hand. His fingers just touched the row of holes, and he felt a draft of cool air coming from them. Moving slowly along the cot, his fingers still touching the holes, he suddenly reached a section where air was being sucked out of the room.

With a grunt he climbed down off the cot and faced the other room. As he did, his eyes blazed and his fists bunched. While he had been inspecting the ventilating system of his prison, three figures had entered the other room.

One he recognized instantly as the Black Hawk. Another, because of surgical instruments which he took out of a small leather case, was obviously an officer in the Black Medical Corps. And the third was some kind of a staff clerk because he carried a notebook and pencil in his hand. All three wore the uniform of the Black Invaders.

Spellbound for the moment, Dusty watched the medical

man turn over the limp body, bare the lad's right arm and administer a hypodermic injection. Almost instantly the President's son sat up on the cot, and his lips began to move. But the thick glass plating cut off all sound from Dusty.

IN THE flicker of a second he knew and understood what this was all about. He wasn't in a prison, he was in a gas cell. And the heavy perfume he smelled was the after effects of the Black's talk-vapor. He was as positive of that, as he was of his own name.

He, Dusty, had already been subjected to the Talk-Vapor. Good God, what had he revealed? No military secrets, of course. He knew none. Yet—

He shuddered as he realized that he could have said certain things about the location of Yank air units—things about the technical details of the Silver Flash, which the Blacks wanted so much to know—things about his talk with the President— the President's fears and worries.

And now those devils were probing the brain of the President's son. What the lad could reveal, Dusty didn't know. But he must be telling them something important for the Black staff clerk was writing furiously in his notebook.

With a curse, Dusty leaped for the glass wall, and smashed his fists against it.

"You rats!" he howled. "You dirty rats—leave that kid alone. By God, I'll—"

He finished the rest in a groan. The three Blacks had their backs to him, and they didn't even hear him. He might just as well have been yelling at the moon.

...AN IRON FIST WITH ONE HUNDRED AND EIGHTY FIVE POUNDS OF BONE AND MUSCLE BEHIND IT CAUGHT HIM SQUARE ON HIS JAW.

And then as he saw the medico administer a second injection in the lad's arm, saw the lad twitched convulsively on the cot, it became more than he could stand. He spun around, picked up his iron cot and, using it as a battering ram, he charged straight at the glass wall.

The wall smashed and fell outward with a crash like the roar of salvo fire. The Blacks, not knowing what had happened, ducked instinctively. And in those few split seconds allowed, Dusty went through the jagged gap in the glass wall and hurled himself on the nearest Black.

It was the medico. He had only time to scream and fling up his hands before an iron fist with one hundred eighty-five pounds of bone and muscle behind it caught him square on his jaw. The medico went flying over backward to thud against the floor and lay still.

Dusty spun around and leaped at the staff clerk. His blood danced as his fists crashed against yielding flesh. That the blows were being returned, he didn't even notice.

Then the Black staff clerk caught a right cross and it was all over. He went down like a felled ox, and lay stretched on the door cold.

Panting, his nose bleeding, Dusty stood over him, glaring. Then he suddenly remembered the most important enemy of all—the Black Hawk.

He spun around, expecting to see a deadly purple stream spewing out from the Black Hawk's gas gun. But—he faced a blank wall. The man had disappeared. As Dusty's eyes fell on the steel door, his lips twisted back in a grimace of scorn. So, the Hawk didn't take chances with his own hide!

Reasonably sure that the door was locked, he nevertheless walked over to it and tried the knob. Just as he thought, it was securely fastened; he couldn't even turn the knob. Returning to the prostrate forms on the floor, he searched them for weapons, found none, and gave his attention to the President's son.

THE LAD had sunk back on the cot, and was lying there, eyes closed and chest heaving. Dusty shook him gently.

"Come on, Charlie," he called out, "That's the boy—breathe deep!"

But the child's only response was to tremble violently, and gulp for air. The pilot tried slapping him sharply on both cheeks. As though some inner spell had been broken, his eyelids flickered. At first he stared dully at Dusty. Then wild fear leaped into his eyes and he shrank back against the wall.

"Easy does it, Charlie," smiled Dusty. "I won't hurt you. I'm your friend—an American. How do you feel, son?"

Large blue eyes regarded him with fearful suspicion. Then gradually the fear disappeared.

"Who are you?"

Dusty told him, and sat down on the edge of the cot.

"Now, don't worry, Charlie. I won't let them hurt you any more. I'll get you out of here, and take you back to your father."

"But you can't!" the youngster half sobbed. "My father is dead. They—they told me so. And they showed me his body, too."

Dusty started violently.

"When did they do that?"

"Yesterday noon, I think it was," came the faint reply. "They—"

"You're sure it was your father?" the pilot cut in. "You really saw him?"

"Well, I'm pretty sure it was my father. They didn't let me get close to him—he was on a bed and I couldn't see much of his face. But he looked like my father."

Dusty scowled at the floor. What the hell were these Blacks up to now?

"Listen, Charlie," he said softly. "They lied to you. That wasn't your father you saw. It was a man they tried to make you believe was your father.

"Charlie, your dad is alive. I was talking with him not over ten hours ago. He's alive and hoping you'll be a brave fellow. That's the truth, lad, on my word of honor. So keep your chin up, everything is going to turn out all right. You just wait and see."

A slight bit of color seeped into the young face, and a defiant little chin jutted out.

"I'm not afraid of them!" said the boy stoutly. "I told them so, too. They're not going to get me to talk, not even if they try a thousand years."

"Listen, Charlie," asked Dusty quickly, "what did they try to make you say? What did they ask you?"

The child puckered his brows and scratched his head.

"Oh, a lot of things about the places my father visits in Washington," he answered. "And all about who comes to see him. But mostly they kept asking me about a man they called Agent 10. Some kind of a secret service man, I guess.

"They said that he killed my father, and that they were trying to find him and turn him over to the American police. But if my dad is alive, then that isn't so, and they wouldn't do that anyway, would they, Captain Ayres?"

Dusty didn't answer. Agent 10? The Blacks wanted to know about Agent 10? Then they didn't—

He cut off the rest, and peered hard at the President's son.

"What did they ask you about Agent 10?"

"Oh, lots of things. Who he was, and what he looked like, and if my father had got any reports that he was dead. Things like that. I didn't know anything about it. I never heard of any Agent 10. But even if I did know—I wouldn't tell them!

"Gee, Captain Ayres, did you knock those fellows out like that?"

Charlie pointed a small hand excitedly at the two forms on the floor, and his blue eyes blazed with admiration.

"They got in our way, son," Dusty said. "And we'll do the same to any others who get in our way, won't we? Now, just lie back and get some rest I won't leave you. I'm just going to sit here and think about our next move."

"But, suppose some of the others come back?" Charlie asked fearfully. "There's hundreds of them around. I saw them."

"We'll just wait until they come," Dusty smiled, "Now, you take it easy."

With a smile of complete faith and trust, the lad sank back on the cot. But he did not close his eyes. He kept them riveted on Dusty's face, frank hero worship glowing in their blue depths. IN CONTRAST, Dusty's eyes went hard as he sat motionless glaring down at the floor. This new angle baffled him more than ever. Why were the Black Invaders going to such extreme measures to find out about a dead man? And how had they come to know about the existence of Agent 10 in the first place? Had Horner, while under the Talk-Vapor, told them the truth? Was Agent 10—?

Suddenly, Dusty stiffened. A stinging acrid smell was in his nose, and his eyes were starting to water. He glanced sidewise at the boy and saw tears trickling down over his pale cheeks. At that moment the lad coughed, and gasped for breath.

"Captain Ayres—Captain Ayres, what is happening? I can't breathe!"

Another spell of violent coughing wracked the child's body from head to toe. Dusty tried to talk to him, but his words choked in his own throat.

"It's all right, Charlie," he gagged, "I won't let—them—hurt you!"

Charlie writhed with fright.

"Captain, I can't brea—"

The rest was lost in a choking gurgle, and the boy fell over on his side.

With a choked curse, Dusty staggered to the door, jerked and tugged on the knob, but to no avail. The steel door didn't budge a fraction of an inch. Frantically he whirled, searching the walls for some kind of a window, that perhaps he had overlooked. But he saw none.

Then, as his eyes raised to the row of holes, his heart skipped a beat. No air was coming through them now. Instead a thick yellowish vapor was pouring into the room.

Throat bursting, lungs bursting for air, he stumbled back to the cot. With arms that felt like lead bars, he tugged and pulled the President's son down onto the floor. From a long way off he heard his own gasping voice.

"Way down, Charlie, way down. Only breathe a little at a time, lad!"

He did not realize that the lad was beyond hearing, so he kept calling out words of encouragement. His voice grew weaker and weaker, until it became merely incoherent whispering, and then faded out.

One arm flung protectingly across the boy, he stared watery-eyed at the rear wall. Though his whole body was numb and lifeless, his brain, strangely enough, was as clear as crystal. And like well-drilled soldiers on parade, every important event in his life went marching in front of him. It was as though he were reliving his span, from babyhood to the present moment.

And then, when the parade had passed, a curtain of darkness swept slowly down over his brain.

CHAPTER 8
FIRE-EYES

AS INSENSIBILITY had come upon Dusty, so did consciousness return, slowly and unhurried. Objects weaved twisted before his eyes, and then stabilized themselves.

He was sitting in the middle of a high-domed room. In front

of him was an empty chair set up on a small dais. Beyond the chair, and high up on the wall, was a row of square windows through which the pale glow of early dawn now filtered.

To the left and to the right, extending the full length of the flanking walls, were what looked to him like courtroom jury boxes. At the moment they were filled with cruel-eyed figures, each one garbed in the close-fitting, jet black uniform of the Invaders. And every pair of eyes was fixed steadfastly on him.

With a desperate effort, he swept them with a steely glance and tried to turn in the chair. But he couldn't, and it was then he realized that stout leather straps bound him. There was one stretched across his chest. Two others pinned his arms to the arms of the chair. And two more jack-knifed off the lower part of his legs under the seat.

So tight were the straps, and so uncomfortable his position, that even the turning of his head caused a hundred hidden demons to hammer at his muscles. With a tiny gasp of pain, he let his body relax, and sat motionless, staring dully before him at the empty chair on the dais.

A moment later there was a movement behind him, a harsh chuckle, and presently he saw the lean, angular figure of the Black Hawk. Crooked lips curled back in a smile, and fang teeth glistened.

"So, the tiger cub does not like its new cage, eh?"

Dusty glared at him scornfully.

"And the rat runs from the fight as usual!" he countered.

The Black threw back his head and roared with laughter. It was almost a minute before he stopped.

"My compliments, Captain," he said with a mock bow. "A very clever retort, even for an American. But let me remind you, that there is an ancient proverb which goes, 'Energy spent where not needed is but casting one's wealth into the sea.' Why then should I waste strength subduing you, when but the turning of a valve would do the same thing?"

"You wouldn't," Dusty snapped at him. "You'd only fight with an eleven-year-old kid. What have you done with him, anyway?"

"I'm afraid you are not in a position to be too belligerent," the other cut in harshly. "But if it helps your role of misguided protector, let me tell you that the boy is quite alive. That gas was not deadly. Simply a type formulated to quell certain annoyances."

Dusty gave him a long searching look, and felt just a little bit relieved. The other doubtlessly saw the relief in his face, for he nodded in additional confirmation.

"No, Captain. The boy is not dead—yet!"

Before Dusty could think of a reply, a bell clanged in some other part of the building. The effect upon those in the high-domed room was electrical. Instantly everyone stiffened to attention, eyes fixed straight ahead. Dusty felt a strange and eerie sensation, and for no reason that he could explain to himself at the moment, he sucked in his breath and held it expectantly.

A moment later, a door in the far corner of the room opened and two giant Black soldiers marched stiffly inside. Three paces inside the door they clicked to a halt, stepped smartly three paces to the left and right, then half turned and faced each other.

As the last click of their polished boot heels died away to an echo, the silence of a tomb settled over the big room. A great desire to look at the others surged over Dusty. But he could not have moved his eyes at that moment even if it should cost him his life. As though held by some secret magnetic vise, his eyes remained glued on the open doorway.

AND THEN, after seconds of intense suspense came the slow scuff-scuff of walking boots, and a great black figure filled the entire doorway.

Instantly a thunderous shout rocked the room from floor to domed ceiling. To Dusty's stunned ears it sounded like—

"*He-e-e-e la-a-a zo!*" With the major emphasis on the last syllable.

Every nerve and muscle in his body was twanging with excitement. And well they should, for that great black figure in the doorway was the earthly counterpart of the god Mars. Fire-Eyes, commander in chief of the Black Invaders—Fire-Eyes, self-styled Emperor of the World!

A mountain of jet black which seemed to literally dwarf everything else in the room—a mountain of black magnetism that held every human in its presence in a trance.

That was Dusty's first impression of the barbarian war lord who sought to smash civilization into the dust.

And then, little by little, Dusty's spellbound eyes became conscious of details. He saw the thick, shiny, black leather half-boots, the coarse black dragoon breeches which bagged down over the boot tops, the skin-fitting black tunic of the same material, which carried no insignia save the braided, green-gold shoulder straps. And above the high tunic collar was a close-fitting mask of dark green. It was made of some stiff material, perhaps even metal, for it did not wave or flap outward as the man walked forward.

Topping the green mask, a black skull cap hung down over the back of his neck like a sun protector worn by those who spend their lives on the burning deserts. And the hands! They too were covered. Covered by glossy black gauntlets which extended halfway up the forearm and then flared out.

From head to toe not a square inch of the man himself was visible. Nothing except the eyes. And yet, no man could call them eyes. There was nothing human about them; no whites, no lids, no lashes. They were but balls of fire which blazed out from behind the slits in the stiff green mask.

With measured steps, the terrible figure approached the dais chair. The giant guards, reduced to pigmy size by comparison, followed three paces behind, their cruel razor-edged faces like chiseled granite. Mounting the dais, Fire-Eyes paused, motionless, for a fraction of a second, then he raised his right, gloved hand, palm on a line with his shoulder, and faced forward.

"He-e-e la-a-a zo!"

The strange roar boomed about the room, feet and chairs scraped against the floor, and all present sat down. But sound only told Dusty that all had seated themselves. For his eyes were still glued to the gigantic man in front of him. Like the small animal held powerless by the beady, gleaming eyes of the cobra, he sat rigid and unblinking.

"You are the American airman known as Captain Ayres?"

The mask didn't even flutter, and the grating voice was as clear as though there were no mask covering the lips.

Dusty said nothing. He couldn't. He was too weak to speak. The sudden words had snapped the spell, and taut nerves were relaxing in rebellious freedom. Like a revived drowning man his aching lungs gulped in blessed air, and the blood tingled through his veins.

"Answer me!"

Like thundering guns the words roared out from behind the mask. But Dusty didn't even flinch. The spell was broken—this thing in front of him was no longer a mirage of horror—it was a human being, a man with flesh, blood and bones like himself. Hardly realizing what he was doing, Dusty laughed.

"What do you think?" he said.

The snarl of an enraged tiger blasted against his ears, and he saw the Black Hawk leaping for him, one hammer-head fist upraised. Instinctively he braced himself for the crushing blow.

But the blow never fell. One sharp word in a strange language barked out from behind the green mask, and the Black Hawk dropped his hand and went back a step as though he had been hit. Bowing low from the waist, he retreated out of Dusty's view.

The pilot grinned at Fire-Eyes.

"Thanks."

"Silence!" the other thundered back. "And I speak to you

now. There is one American we wish to find, he is known as Agent 10. Where is he?"

Dusty curbed the sudden start the question gave him. He fought to keep his face blank.

"Why ask me? I thought you devils knew everything!"

Whether or not the smart-alecky reply angered the figure behind the mask, there was no way of telling.

However, the words which came next were calm and deliberate.

"Agent 10 of your Intelligence Department aided you in making your escape ten days ago, Captain Ayres. Since then he has continued to be troublesome, I offer you your life—if you tell me who he is and what he looks like, and you may return to your own country unharmed."

POKER-FACED, DUSTY stared at the green mask with its two balls of fire and said nothing, but his brain was spinning in a mad whirl of joy. One man, and a dead man at that, was checkmating the Black Invaders. Long ago a famous general had said, "Keep the enemy worried, and you have already won half your battle."

The truth of those long forgotten words was striking home now. The Black Invaders were worried. They wanted Agent 10, and wanted him bad. God rest that gallant soldier's heart, he'd probably jabbed many thorns in their sides, and Fire-Eyes didn't know that he was dead! Chalk one up for the Yank side!

"You heard me, Captain Ayres?"

Some of the grating harshness had faded from the voice. Dusty gave him an agate stare.

"I heard you."

The gloved fingers drummed softly on the arms of the chair.

"It is a life for a life, captain. And life is very sweet. Where is Agent 10?"

Dusty tried a long shot for no particular reason other than to possibly add worry to worry.

"Probably right in this room," he said easily. "That wouldn't be difficult for him."

The drumming fingers doubled into fists, but the rest of the man was motionless.

"Ah, so he is not dead?"

The question and the meaning behind it smote Dusty between the eyes, and his heart sank.

"How do I know?" said the Yank quickly. "I'm only a pilot."

He wasn't sure, but he thought a faint chuckling sound came out from behind the green mask.

"I change my question, Captain Ayres," said Fire-Eyes, suddenly leaning forward. "Is this Agent 10 dead or alive, as far as you know?"

Out of sheer desperation Dusty took the middle track.

"I don't know," he said.

As he spoke the last word, Fire-Eyes' right hand raised up in some sort of a signal. Instantly Dusty heard a soft movement behind him, and a split second later his body was consumed with horrible pain as the leather straps were jerked tighter than ever.

He felt as though his arms and legs were being pulled clear of his body. Sweat poured off him, and a red blur filmed his

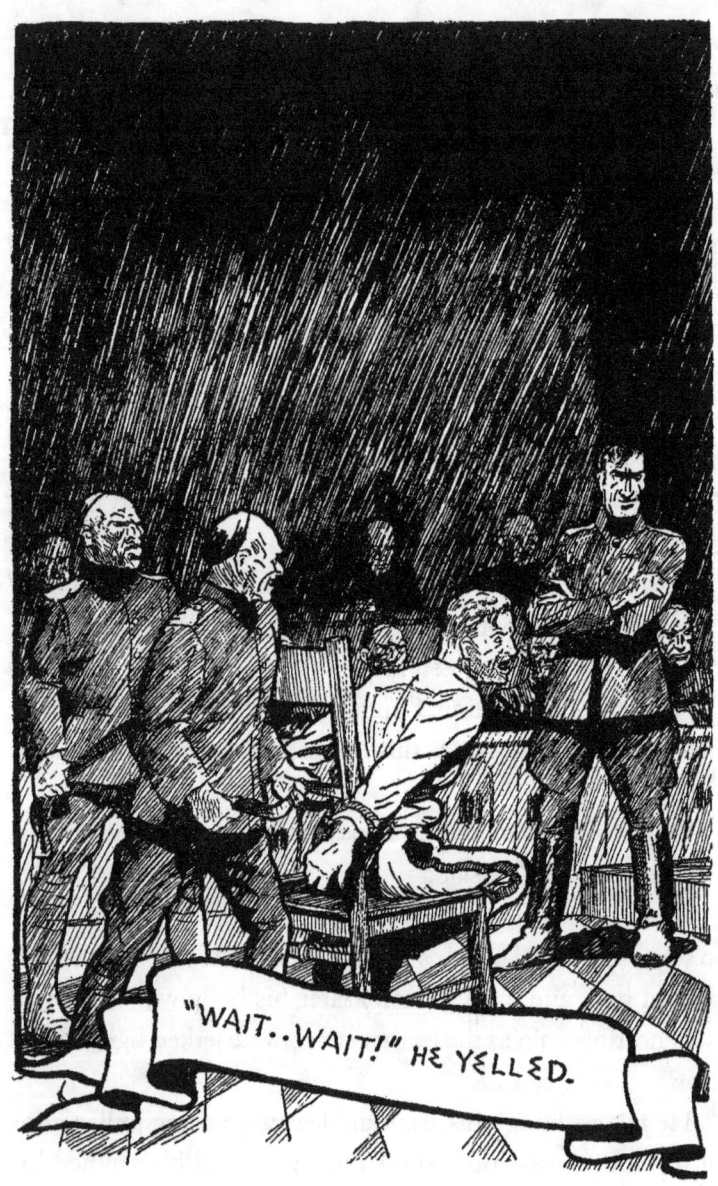

"WAIT..WAIT!" HE YELLED.

eyes. But with clenched teeth he called upon every bit of will-power and resistance that was his.

"Answer me, Captain Ayres! Dead or alive?"

The voice came as booming guns in the distance. And his answer like the crackle of machine-gun fire just as far distant.

"I—don't—know!"

The straps were drawn tighter and Dusty's brain hammered and pounded inside his head. And then, as he felt himself slipping down into the void of unconsciousness, the straps were suddenly slackened.

Choking, fighting for breath, he slumped backward, not caring a damn what happened next. But youth, fighting youth, is tough, and little by little strength flowed back into that throbbing body.

"You have courage, Captain. And to one who has courage, pain means very little—life, too. But you have answered my question. You have answered by giving me no answer. Agent 10 is still alive. He must be, for only a fool would suffer to conceal the fate of a dead man."

Still weak from the pain, Dusty was nevertheless able to thrill inwardly at Fire-Eyes' statement. They thought Agent 10 was alive. Thank God for that. Each passing moment would increase their worry and uneasiness. And when an army commander is like that, his battle judgment is as far from being at par. Good old Agent 10—God bless his memory, he lived in mystery and died the same way.

But Fire-Eyes was speaking again.

"Who is he, and what does he look like, captain? You saw him ten days ago—what did he look like?"

"Like any of your rats," the pilot got out weakly.

"And who is he?"

"I don't know!" Dusty shouted.

There followed a long silence. Then presently Fire-Eyes spoke again. His voice was like the hiss of a snake.

"I think you lie, captain. And I shall find out. You have courage, and pain means little. Let us see how you react when others are in pain!"

AGAIN THE right, gloved hand came up in silence. A minute of silence passed, and then the blood in Dusty's veins boiled over with savage rage. Two Black guards had entered through the end door, and were half carrying between them the white-faced, limp figure of the President's son.

"Damn your soul, Fire-Eyes!" yelled the pilot. "Leave him alone. I tell you—I swear to you, he knows nothing. Do you hear? He knows nothing. Good Lord, he's just a kid!"

"Exactly!" the Black commander boomed back. "He doesn't know anything, but you do, Captain!"

Cursing out his wrath, Dusty sat helpless while the guards shoved the President's son into a chair and bound his thin arms behind him. Too utterly spent to hold his head up, the lad let it sink down on his chest. But for his arms linked around the back of the chair, he would have toppled over on his face on the floor.

The sight was like a knife slashing Dusty's heart to shreds, and it was several minutes before Fire-Eyes' voice registered on his consciousness.

"And now, Captain, if you understand, perhaps you will answer my question."

"I don't know!" answered the pilot thickly. "I tell you I don't know anything about any Agent 10."

"And yet a man we fully believe to be this Agent 10 saved your life, eh?" came back the purring comment. "Very well, Captain, I gave you your chance. Now—watch!"

Strange words rattled out from behind the green mask. Instantly one of the guards jerked open a small trap door in the floor, and stuck his hand through the opening. When he pulled it out, the hand held what looked like a soldering iron—an electric one, for a coil of heavy cable extended from the handle down into the floor opening.

Walking over to the limp boy, the guard held the thing loosely in his right hand, and looked at Fire-Eyes. The commander in chief of the Black Invaders slowly turned in his chair and nodded.

There came the click of a switch, a singing hiss, and a tiny pin point of blue flame spurted out from the blunt end of the iron. Through horror-gripped eyes, Dusty saw the blue pin point of flame move closer and closer to the bloodless cheek of the President's son.

The heat from the thing must have jerked the lad back to partial consciousness, for he raised his head slowly. Then sunken blue eyes saw the flame, inches from them, and moving ever closer to burn out their depths. The lad shrank back, tried to cry out, but got only as far as a gasp before he fainted.

With his free hand the guard took hold of the child's hair, and forced his head back. The blue pin point moved closer, and then something inside of Dusty gave way, and he could stand the hideous sight no longer.

"Wait—wait!" he bellowed, writhing against the straps, and totally oblivious of the pain. "Don't—don't, for God's sake. I'll tell you!"

A sharp word from Fire-Eyes and the guard let the boy's head and stepped back.

"Well, Captain Ayres, what are you going to tell us?"

Even now, when his mind was in such turmoil, Dusty could not help but bristle at the undercurrent of bland triumph in the Black commander's tone. But he checked himself a split second later. Nothing mattered now except to save that boy from further torture.

"The man known as Agent 10 is—dead!" he got out. "He was killed during a raid on what was believed to be your head-quarters. That, on my word of honor, is official. The Department in Washington has received official word of his death. Now, damn you, let that poor boy go!"

Fire-Eyes made no answer. He sat motionless, like a statue of black onyx, orbs of fire blazing out from behind his mask. Then suddenly, he made a waving motion with his left hand. Instantly, two guards picked up the boy, chair and all, and disappeared through the end of the door.

"I do not believe that you lie this time, Captain Ayres!" rasped

Fire-Eyes. "One more question, and be careful, Captain. Who was this Agent 10?"

Dusty hesitated a split second, then thought of that white-faced boy, and groaned.

"Agent 10 was the son of General Horner," he said from between tight lips. "And the finest man God ever made!"

"Ah-h-h!"

The sound was like hissing steam.

"Ah-h-h!" Fire-Eyes repeated. "The son of that fool, eh? That tells me a lot. So the mouse stole the cheese after the trap had been sprung!"

The commander in chief of the Black Invaders leaped from his throne on the dais and stalked swiftly out of the room.

CHAPTER 9
AGENT 10

HARDLY HAD the door closed when the Black Hawk walked around in front of Dusty and stood smirking at him gloatingly.

"Well, my good friend," he purred, "he can make you talk, can he not?"

The Yank gave him a scornful eye.

"Watch out," he grated. "The boss may come back and catch you fumbling the ball again!"

The thrust struck home, and the Hawk's face went livid with rage. He took a step toward Dusty, then shot a quick side glance at the other Blacks in the room, and stopped short.

"It is still much too early for the last laugh, Captain!" he practically hissed out. "I suggest that you be sure to remember this moment—at a certain time in the very near future."

Without waiting for Dusty's reply to that, the Hawk turned his back and snarled out some sharp orders. A moment later there was movement behind Dusty.

Then the leather straps fell away from him. With a stifled groan of relief he stretched his aching legs, and tried to rub the circulation back into his numbed arms.

However, he was not allowed much time for that, for almost immediately fingers of steel gripped both his arms and jerked him up on his feet. Had those fingers let go at that moment, he would have folded up on the floor like an army cot, his legs were so lifeless.

But they did not let go, and with a guard on either side of him, he went slipping and sliding and stumbling toward a door at the end of the room which he had not seen before.

The door led out into a small, open-air courtyard, and the cool freshness of early dawn did more for Dusty at that moment than anything else in the world. It cleared his spinning head, set his heart pounding at maximum power, sending new strength-building blood swirling through his veins.

They took him across the courtyard through another door and along a narrow corridor. At the end of the corridor they went through a third and last door which brought them out onto the edge of a small field.

Having recovered sufficient strength to be able to keep step with the cruel-looking, silent apemen who clutched him, Dusty was able to take in this new scene in detail. The result was a sharp quickening of his pulse, and a feeling of suppressed excitement.

On the far side of the field he saw two of the new sheet-Dural hangars and, though a slight ground mist still hung low, he could distinguish the shapes of two planes lined up in front of the hangars. One, he knew positively, he had seen before. It was the radio ship that had attacked him while he was flying General Horner over the Washington field. But it was the other ship that jerked a gasp from his lips. Never in all his sky career had he ever seen anything like it.

To begin with, the plane was little more than a gigantic flying wing. There was no nacelle or fuselage. The interior of the great wing itself undoubtedly took care of all those requirements. Just above the center of the leading edge was a row of sliding glass windows that permitted entrance to the various compartments in the wing.

Power came from four cowled engines set up on streamlined mountings atop, two on either side of the glass windows. The landing gear was of the conventional streamlined retractable type, with single instead of double wheels. And the tail section was of double fin, elevator and rudder design, connected to the giant wing by the conventional I-shaped outrigger booms.

The only difference from the usual type of outrigger tail sections was that on this plane the trailing edge of the wing was V-shaped so that the point of the V extended back a considerable distance between the two points of attachment of the outrigger booms. The antenna masts were in line in the top center of the wing.

But to Dusty's practiced eye the giant craft, which was painted a brilliant crimson from tip to tip, represented the very last word in streamlined effect. Nothing save the mounted engines, and two short, stubby radio masts, marred the otherwise perfect air-flow equalities of the wing.

Yet with a thrill of admiration, there also came to Dusty a faint tremor of horror, for he knew that he was looking at man's most terrible weapon of aerial destruction—a radio-controlled bomber, that when fully loaded could be sent thundering down into a great city and wipe out a square mile of buildings in one roar of flame and sound. Opposing airmen would be practically helpless against it, because to shoot it down would bring the same terrible result, though perhaps not on the original objective.

And then, as the guards jerked Dusty behind a row of small buildings that hid the planes from view, complete realization came to him with startling suddenness. That bomber—that gigantic craft of crimson doom, was intended to be the flying grave of the President's son! That was the plane Fire-Eyes would send crashing into the national capitol at Washington. And that radio ship would act as the master control.

Yes, Horner's guess had probably been right. The pilot of that strato-radio ship had flown over Washington yesterday in order to acquaint himself with the layout of the city—the city he had received orders to destroy!

With a groan, Dusty tried to argue himself out of such a

belief. The Blacks would be fools to waste such a beautiful and powerful craft. Fire-Eyes' threat to the President had only been a bluff. He wouldn't throw away a craft like that radio bomber.

He wouldn't?

The thought came back to mock Dusty. Hell, to hear that war-devil talk was to realize that the very words, waste and sacrifice, meant absolutely nothing to him. That demon had but one terrible thought behind his blazing eyes, and that was, to destroy the world and make himself emperor of a crumbled civilization, no matter what the cost!

STILL BATTLING the inevitable truth, Dusty suddenly found himself being thrust into a room which was bare save for a cot and a single chair. Too weak to resist, he allowed the guards to practically hurl him across the room and onto the cot. Checking his movement just in time to avert a nasty crash against the wall, he sank down on the cot.

He stared dully at the guards as they took up their positions, one on either side of the door. Arms folded across their broad chests, they stood there like two dumb mutes, beady black eyes fixed steadfastly on space.

As the minutes dragged by, Dusty weighed his chances of a sudden charge and attempt to snatch the gas guns which dangled temptingly from the right hip of each Black. But when the weighing was done, the net result was zero minus.

Sane reason forced him to realize that he'd take just two steps, not even that many, perhaps, and then he'd be smashed flat like a fly caught against the wall. This was one moment when being a damned fool wouldn't net him a single thing.

Nevertheless, the fighter in him refused to give up, and, though appearing not to do so, he kept his eyes glued on the guards and slowly inched forward on the edge of the cot and braced himself to spring.

But he didn't spring, for a few moments later the door opened and a third Black guard shouldered into the room. The other two glanced at him out the corner of their eyes and grunted something. The third guard answered, and fixed his piercing eyes on Dusty.

Steeling himself, the Yank returned the look, glare for glare. Presently the newcomer's lips twisted into a half smirk and he turned to the other two.

And what happened next was a display of man-made action, executed almost faster than the human eye could follow.

The third guard's right hand whipped down and up like a streak of light. As though by magic, a gas gun appeared in the hand. There was a faint hiss, and a tiny purple stream clouded over the face of the guard on the left side of the door.

Hardly seeming to move at all, the Black with the gas gun pivoted around to the other guard, whose hand was already clutching his gun. But he never got it off its hook. A second purple stream caught him square in the mouth, and he crumpled up.

And at that moment came the fastest action of all. The newcomer's arms spread-eagled out, and caught both toppling over guards. Then slowly he eased them to the floor, snatched up their gas guns, and whirled on Dusty.

Instinctively, the Yank pilot braced himself as he saw the gun leveled at him. Then he looked beyond the gas gun, at the face of the Black who was holding it, and gasped hoarsely. The Black's lips were drawn back in a wide grin.

And then, a dead man spoke.

"Howdy, Ayres! Remember me?"

Utter amazement clamped Dusty's tongue in his throat. He felt sure that he had never seen this cruel-faced figure before, yet there was something about the man, the greeting perhaps, that was like a flash of light down the dark hall of memory. And then, with disbelief in his voice, he spoke.

"Your—You are Ag—"

The other's quick nod stopped him.

"Right, Ayres. Still alive and kicking. But I had to die for a while—absolutely necessary."

"But your fa—" Dusty checked himself in time. "But X-34," he corrected, "received official confirmation of your death. He said that one of the other agents had sent it through."

"I know," Agent 10 nodded with a sad smile. "I sent it through myself. I had to. But X-34 told you, about me, eh—who I was? I heard you confess my identity in that council room just now."

Dusty flushed to the ears.

"I believed you dead," he said thickly. "And, hell, that kid, I—"

He finished with a shrug.

"Don't blame you, Ayres," smiled the other. "I would have done the same thing, damn their black hearts. So forget it. We've got too much to do, to worry about things that have already happened."

"Right!" nodded Dusty, starting for the door. "Let's get started pronto."

Agent 10 grabbed him.

"Whoa! Not so fast," he hissed. Now, listen. Though you may not think so, I believe we've got Fire-Eyes walking in circles. Because of a few lucky breaks, I seem to be the only Yank agent who has been able to toss a monkey wrench into the works.

"A week ago, when we made that raid on what we thought was his H.Q., I came so close to being tripped up and unfaced, as you might put it, that it wasn't even funny.

"You see, they found out about the existence of an Agent 10 shortly after the Duluth show. How, don't ask me. But they did, nevertheless, and ever since they've been sitting up nights figuring out a million ways to trip me up, and plant a nice little bullet where it would do the most good.

"Well, anyway, they came damned close to doing it. So there was only one way out left for me—to make them think I was dead. I sent that message to my father through certain channels I knew the Blacks were tapping.

"That gave me a breathing spell, and I set to work to find out where Fire-Eyes was. You see, I'd thought I knew, but that raid proved me wrong."

The man paused for breath, noted Dusty's eyes fixed on the door.

"We've got a few minutes," he said calmly. "We won't be busted in on for a while. They've gone to feed their ugly faces, and hold a general pow-wow."

119

The unhurried coolness of the man was a tonic to Dusty's jangled nerves.

"Okay, iceberg," he grinned. "You were saying?"

"That I set out to find Fire-Eyes," continued the other. "And I succeeded. Believe it or not, his headquarters are right here, some fifty miles west of Chatham, New Brunswick. Less than forty miles from the Maine border.

"No, you don't catch Fire-Eyes taking chances. If things got too hot, he could hop off and be with his North Atlantic fleet within the hour. But that's beside the point. I trailed him here, got all the dope I needed for another raid, and prepared a code message for X-34."

THE AGENT stopped abruptly, and bitter disappointment and anger flooded his lean, homely face.

"And that," he went on a moment later, "was the dumbest stunt a man could have pulled. It wiped out every damned bit of work I'd accomplished. In short, they got hold of the message. It's a mystery to me how they did it. But as I've told you before, these rats just aren't human. They could make the Sphinx talk!

"Well, anyway, as far as they were concerned, Agent 10 was still alive, and that sent them haywire. It also put dynamite under my feet. I decided that to remain was simply asking for a bullet in the back, and so, I was ready to sneak back into the States when, bang!—I learned about the kidnapping of the President's son, and what they intended to do. I couldn't go then. So here I am."

"But I don't get the picture," said Dusty, as the other stopped.

"If Fire-Eyes knew that you were still alive, why did he keep asking me whether you were alive or dead?"

"Don't you get it?" the other scowled. "He got one report that I was dead, and another that I was alive. He couldn't decode the message he intercepted. It's a choice to make.

"And here's the main idea. I know damned well that he couldn't decode the message he intercepted. It's a code the Devil himself couldn't figure out. But for the sake of argument, let us say that he did decode it, and he learned that this mysterious Agent 10 knew of his H.Q.

"Okay, get the reaction in his mind? Simply that he began to wonder if this Agent 10 had sent other messages through—messages that he hadn't picked up. Did the Yanks know where he was?

"That's the thought that lost him plenty sleep, or else I'm a liar! You see, with everything going his way, the President's son in his hands, opportunity to crash down on the very nerve center of our country, and zowie—he intercepts a message sent to X-34 right from his own H.Q., and signed by a pest he believed dead!"

"I get you," nodded Dusty. "But all that hasn't stopped his dirty work. He tripped your dad and learned about me. And then he tripped me up. Or rather, that yellow rat, the Hawk, did. And if those two planes I just saw on the other side of the field mean anything, he's planning to carry out his murdering raid on Washington."

"Correct," Agent 10 replied. "But only partly so. That raid

121

was originally scheduled to take place last night. At the very time the fake prisoner exchange was being made!"

Dusty gasped. "That's the kind of rats they are," the other grated. "But, it was postponed until Fire-Eyes could make sure that his own skin was safe. And that, my lad, is one thing I've found out about this murdering Emperor of the world.

"When it comes to a case of danger to his own hide, he's the yellowest of the yellow. He'll save his skin before anything else. And, I'll wager you my life that if he were sure that word of his location had got through to Washington, he'd light out from here so fast that you wouldn't even realize he'd gone. That's one of his mysterious characteristics. Even those closest to him do not know anything. And he trapped you, and forced just enough out of you to mix him up more than ever.

"Believe me, Ayres, fear for his own hide has got him, and until he finds out for sure, he's not going to make a move. The President's son is his ace in the hole, and he doesn't dare play it—yet!"

The emphasis that went with the last word sent an eerie chill tingling down Dusty's spine. He looked searchingly into the other's eyes, almost hoping that he'd read there the answer to the all-important question—what was the next move?

But, he didn't, and suddenly Agent 10 leaned over, glanced at his wrist watch, and grunted.

"Still a few minutes left," he said aloud. "Now, in case I've missed some parts of the general picture, tell me quickly your side of it."

In short snappy sentences Dusty related every detail from

the moment when he had read the crazy search order in Major Drake's office, right up to the time Agent 10 had busted into the room.

THE INTELLIGENCE man listened in keen, thoughtful silence. But when Dusty finished, he nodded his head slowly and a wide grin of satisfaction curled his lips back. But Dusty frowned.

"Listen, you grinning tower of ice!" he got out irritably. "What the hell is there to grin at? Personally, I think I'd rather be here than in the President's shoes, right now. If you'd seen that damn lying sky sign, and didn't know the truth, what—"

He bit off the rest as Agent 10 continued to grin, and added to Dusty's annoyance by shaking his head from side to side.

"Well?" demanded Dusty. "Spill it!"

"You pilots!" grunted the man. "Hellions in the air, but like old women when you're on the ground. Easy, lad—no offense meant, really.

"But, let us say that the country is on its ear—that is, lying propaganda bunk has gotten under their skin. Well what could be better than to prove it all unfounded? The result couldn't possibly be anything but redoubled faith in the wisdom of the government at present in Washington."

All of which impressed Dusty not very much.

"Prove it unfounded?" he echoed in a rasping voice. "How, damn it—how? By God, wait—those planes on the field—we could—"

Agent 10 nodded excitedly.

"Just what I meant," he said. "Now look, the Blacks are having

123

a pow-wow and feeding their faces. The President's son is in a shack less than a hundred yards from here, with a single guard in his room. You have two guards over you, only they happen to be dead.

"And on the other side of the field is a nice little high-altitude radio plane, and a radio-controlled bomber… and no other planes. The bomber is too big and clumsy, I think—so you can pilot the radio ship, and the President's son and I will go along as passengers. In three hours, barring accidents, we should be looking at the smile of joy on the President's face."

Agent 10 finished with a nothing-to-it gesture of his hands. But, although the blood beat faster through Dusty's veins, he stood scowling at the floor. There was an angle that bothered him.

"What's the matter, Ayres? No like?"

The sharp question jerked Dusty up straight.

"What about the possibility of them spotting me?" he asked. "This uniform of mine—and they're not blind, you know."

Agent 10 snorted.

"Of course, they're not blind, but they won't see your uniform! You're changing with one of these clucks on the floor. And when we pick up the boy, well only be fifty yards from the plane. The hangar guard will simply think we're acting on orders. If he doesn't, well—we'll just make him stop thinking. After that, your flying skill will be our guiding star."

"And how!" grinned Dusty. "Okay, let's go. Here, give me a hand with this tramp's clothes. He seems to be the smallest of the two."

Lips silent and fingers working feverishly, they stripped off the uniform of the dead guard who lay to the right of the door. Two minutes later, Dusty had slipped it on over his own uniform. It was a very bad fit, but there was nothing that could be done about it.

"Set?" grunted Agent 10 finally. And when he got Dusty's nod, "Right, here we go. No, wait. Take this gas gun, just in case. I'll go first. Stick close behind me, keep your head down as much as you can, and let me do all the talking. Thank God, I know their blasted lingo from A to izzard."

A grin and Agent 10 opened the door and stepped through. Hesitating just the fraction of a second to steel himself Dusty shuffled out at his heels.

CHAPTER 10
EAGLE'S TRAP

HAD THE ground he walked upon been strewn with detonating H.E. bombs, Dusty's nerves could not have been more on edge. A million times he had the wild, insane desire to jab Agent 10 in the back and call for more speed.

The Intelligence man was moving at a snail's pace, and to Dusty's way of thinking, wasted seconds and minutes were whizzing past. But each time he managed to curb the fanatical urge and forced himself to plow slowly forward, head down and eyes glued on the polished boot heels of Agent 10.

Inch by inch, foot by foot, and yard by yard they went down a low row of huts. Once, a voice cried out behind them. Dusty's

125

blood froze and it took every ounce of his will-power to stop himself from glancing back over his shoulder.

Whether Agent 10 had heard it or not, he couldn't tell. The Intelligence man kept on shuffling forward, as though he didn't have a care in the world. Holding his breath, and expecting every second to hear the crack of a rifle, and feel the sting of hot steel slapping into his back, Dusty stuck doggedly to his part of the plan.

And then, after at least a thousand years had dragged by, Agent 10 stopped, glanced casually around and spoke softly through lips that did not move.

"The second hut from here, Ayres. Keep right behind me, and have that gas gun ready. That guard must not let out even a yip. Okay, we move on."

Dusty edged closer to Agent 10 as they went through the door. For an instant he caught a glimpse of the President's son lying on a cot. The lad's eyes were closed, and his small body was still as death. And then Dusty jerked his eyes away as a harsh voice snarled something he did not understand. It came from the lips of a big Black guard who stood straddle-legged in front of Agent 10.

The Intelligence man started to reply, then cut it off short. Purple spurted from his gas gun, and the guard crumpled over without a sound, Agent 10 catching him as he fell.

It all happened so fast that Dusty was left standing like a gaping mummy. But, a split second later, death sliced at him and galvanized his doped muscles into furious action. That death was in the form of a second Black guard whom the opening door had concealed. And now he was charging across the room, one big hairy hand tugging at his gas gun.

"God—look out!"

The words were little more than a gasping moan that spilled from Agent 10's lips. His arms filled with the slumping dead-weight of the first guard, the Intelligence man was helpless to snap up his gas gun. And as the agent and his dead burden were between him and the charging Black, Dusty was unable to fire his gun without spewing the deadly fumes into his comrade's face.

All that, he saw and realized in the flash of a split second. Dusty whipped his gun hand forward. The gun flew from his fingers, streaked across less than five feet of air space, and caught the Black square between the eyes. And the very instant Dusty hurled his own body after it. Like a circus acrobat, he curved over Agent 10, struggling to get his arms free, and crashed into the second Black who, partially stunned, was charging blindly forward.

As Dusty's body crashed into him, the forward motion stopped. The Black's gun flew from his fingers and went skidding across the floor, and the man himself staggered back two steps, got his big feet tangled up with each other, and went crashing down with Dusty on top of him.

Hot breath from panting lungs blasted against the Yank's face, and two great arms of steel circled his body and started clamping together. For one awful second Dusty thought that his back had been snapped in two.

Sweat streamed off his forehead, and savage snarls rattled

against his eardrums. Twisting, jerking, butting with his head, he fought desperately to break loose from the band of steel which was caving in his ribs. The room swam before his eyes, and a thousand fire gongs clanged and banged inside his head.

And then suddenly, he was dimly conscious of his right fist smashing against the jaw bone. A white-hot pain raced up his arm. Then another sizzling pain raced up his left arm.

Half blind with pain, his head a canyon of roaring sound, he fought with the fury of a dozen wild cats. Hands grabbed his arms and shoulders, but he knocked them free with his lashing fist. Bang—slam—wham! One hundred eighty-five pounds of seething rage behind each blow. Bang—slam—wham! Take it—and take some more!

"Ayres—Ayres! For God's sake, man, stop!"

Out of a sea of red came the voice. It cut in through his whirling senses, and echoed back. Hands grabbed his wrists and pinned them to his sides. He wrenched and tugged furiously.

"Wait, man, hold it!"

The voice touched a hidden spring in his brain. Almost automatically he relaxed, shook his head, and brushed aside the red haze. Through blinking eyes he saw Agent 10's face close to his.

"Hold it, you damned wildcat!" the man snapped. "He was through long ago."

Frowning, Dusty glanced down at his feet.

Stretched out lifeless was the ape figure of the Black guard. The man's face was no longer ugly-looking. It was worse than that—it was like a big lump of minced steak that had just been put through the grinder.

THE PILOT stared at it for a second or two, then rubbed his bleeding knuckles and grinned. "I feel better," he grunted.

"I should think you would!" snorted Agent 10. "Boy, can you do things when you try! But, come on—we've got to step—and the lad seems done in."

As memory of the President's son returned, Dusty spun around and went over to the cot. The boy's eyes were still closed, but he was breathing easily.

"Asleep," Dusty grunted. "All in, poor little kid. We've got to wake him up."

Several precious seconds flew by before the boy reacted to their gentle shaking, and opened his eyes. He saw Dusty first, recognized him, and grinned faintly. Then as his eyes met Agent 10's they clouded with fear, and his lips trembled.

"Easy, Charlie!" said Dusty sharply. "He's a friend—he's going to help me take you back to your dad. Think you can stand up, son?"

"I think so, sir," the boy smiled bravely.

But the lad had underestimated his condition, and when he got to his feet he swayed crazily and would have toppled over on his face but for Dusty's quick hand.

"Hang on, son, hang on," he said soothingly. "Try and keep your feet moving. We haven't got far to go. You know, the old pep—they can't lick us Yanks. Here, we'll help you. That's the boy—you're doing great. Okay, let's go."

The last was to Agent 10 who had taken hold of the child's

other arm. And with the boy stumbling between them they moved toward the door, through it, and out into the open air.

With Agent 10 acting as guide, they trudged to the end of the hut row and paused long enough for the Intelligence man to peer around the corner.

"All clear," he nodded a moment later. "We'll cut straight across the corner. No, not too fast."

Checking his sudden desire for speed, Dusty dropped back into step with the others, and grimly fixed his eyes on the hangars fifty yards away. Only fifty yards—yet to him they seemed fifty miles.

The bomber and the radio plane were still there. And, as far as he could see, there wasn't the sign of a single hangar guard. Thirty-five yards to go! The blood pounded and danced through his veins. And then his heart went still, as faint, choked words came from the boy's lips.

"I—I—can't! I'm going—to—faint!"

The last word was but a whisper, as the boy became a dead weight between them. Dusty started to speak, but Agent 10 cut him off.

"No use, Ayres, too far gone. We've got to carry him between us—like this."

Bracing themselves, each hooked an arm under the lad's armpits and lifted him so that only the toes of his shoes dragged along the ground. And then, veins bulging at the temples, sweat pouring off their brows, they walked forward the last twenty yards.

At last they reached the glossy fuselage of the radio plane.

"Quick—inside with him!" came Agent 10's hoarse voice.

Dusty released his hold on the boy, reached for the chrome handle of the fuselage door, but never touched it.

Like magic the fuselage door popped open, and a stream of black poured out on top of them. The snarling roar of hell-demons filled the air. Dusty reeled back, tried to snatch for his gas gun, but his right arm was still hooked in the boy's and his clawing fingers grabbed only the loose folds of the Black uniform he wore.

"Lookout, Ayres!"

THE YELL came from Agent 10's lips, and a split second later Dusty heard a low groan. Immediately he was thrown off balance. Agent 10 had suddenly crumpled to the ground, pulled the boy down with him. Unable to get his arm free, Dusty went sprawling down on top of the heap. As he lay gasping for breath, hands clutched him, jerked him to his feet. And it was only then that he was able to distinguish separate faces in the black wave of humanity that virtually swirled all about him.

The first was the face of the Black Hawk, twisted with snarling triumph. And the second—it wasn't a face. It was the stiff green mask of Fire-Eyes himself; the balls of fire behind the slits actually spewing out tongues of white flame.

Helpless in the grip of several Black soldiers, Dusty could only glare back at the two hideous faces leering at him. Then he turned his head and looked down at the ground. Unconsciousness was protecting the President's son from the terror of it all. And unconsciousness had also wrapped its cloak around Agent 10. Flat on his back, arms flung out helplessly, he lay still as the earth itself. And from an ugly gash on his right temple, a tiny trickle of blood oozed down over the ear, dropped off the lobe and seeped into the ground.

The harsh voice of Fire-Eyes made him glance up. "So, you lied, Captain, eh? Agent 10 is not dead—yet!"

"Go to hell!" Dusty snapped.

For an answer, a black-gloved fist flashed through the air and crashed into his face. He forced his lips back in a grin.

"You can still go to hell!"

Fighting to keep the grin on his lips, Dusty waited for the second blow. But it never came. Instead, Fire-Eyes turned and bent his head toward the prostrate Intelligence man. A moment later words came out from behind the mask.

"But the mouse did not wait for the second trap to spring!

"Fool! Did you think that you could defeat me, the great conqueror? Bah! Did you think that I could not guess such a silly plan? And now I shall teach your countrymen a lesson. Now, your President shall witness my power!"

Spinning half around, the giant man rasped out a string of strange words.

Instantly Black soldiers laid hold of Agent 10 and the President's son. Carrying them like sacks of meal across their shoulders, they tramped over to the crimson bomber.

At a nod from Fire-Eyes, the two holding Dusty forced him to stumble drunkenly over to the bomber also. He saw the soldiers bind the arms and legs of the boy and Agent 10, and then hoist them up through a trap door in the center underside part of the huge crimson plane.

A moment later, he saw their white faces through the windows in the leading edge of the wing. And from the way the Black soldiers were bending over them he realized with sinking heart that they were being lashed fast against the rear wall of the forward compartment.

A HARSH chuckle at his side caused him to turn his head. The Hawk stood there, watching him with gloating eyes. The Black nodded toward the plane.

"A perfect touch, eh, my friend?" he leered. "Our great leader always gives a man his most desired wish. And those two desired to return to their own country. Well, they shall!"

"Call these dogs off and I'll kill you with my bare hands!" The Yank blazed.

But the Black Hawk simply shook his head, and smiled.

Before he could speak, the Black soldiers came out of the crimson bomber and slammed the trap door up in place. Fire-Eyes, who had been standing in front of the plane, watching them, turned away and signaled to a group in mechanic's overalls.

Like puppets, the men scrambled up ladders to the top of the wing, and started cranking the motors. Seconds later, all four propellers were turning over lazily. The ladders were taken away and the great craft wheeled around, nose toward the takeoff ramp.

As they turned the ship around, Dusty took one last look at the row of windows. Agent 10 had regained consciousness, and through the thick glass, his face was visible. Dusty saw his lips

AS THEY TURNED THE SHIP AROUND, DUSTY TOOK ONE LAST LOOK...

draw back in a smile of defiance, and farewell. Then, the turning plane hid him from view.

The Yank ace battled desperately to keep back the tears of bitter defeat that crowded to his eyes. Through a blur he saw a Black pilot climb into the radio plane, start its single engine, and go streaking across the field and high up into the morning sky.

As the plane took off, a Black soldier rolled a portable radio set out of the hangar, clamped phones on his ears, adjusted the small directional loop antenna, and busied himself spinning dial knobs. A few moments later, he looked at Fire-Eyes, nodded his head, and raised his right hand to his right shoulder, palm outward, in the peculiar salute of the Invaders.

The commander-in-chief returned the salute, and half turning, signaled the Hawk to his side. For several seconds they conversed in low tones. Watching the motions of the Hawk's hands, Dusty guessed that the man was pleading for something. Several times Fire-Eyes shook his head. Then, suddenly, he nodded and waved the Hawk from his presence.

Eyes gleaming with joy, lips curled back over fang teeth in what was supposed to be a smile, the Hawk snapped an order to a soldier.

The man disappeared into the hangar, and reappeared a moment later carrying a parachute vest and pack. Saluting, he handed it to the Hawk.

Still holding that hideous smile on his face, the Black ace pilot walked up to Dusty and held out the vest-pack.

"As I said, Captain," he leered, "you shall not die but live and remember. To us you are harmless, and it is my personal desire that you live to remember me. Our great commander has just now granted me my wish."

Rough hands seized Dusty, stripped the Black uniform from him, shoved his arms through the holes in the chute vest, and strapped the whole thing in place around the upper back of his body.

At a nod from the Hawk, the guards lifted him clear of the ground, carried him under the wing of the crimson plane, pulled down a trap door in the V of the wing, and hurled him bodily into a steel-walled compartment. A split second later, the steel trap clanked shut, and from the other side he heard the Hawk's rasping chuckle.

"A pleasant voyage, my friend. Be sure to think of me—and explain everything to the good General Horner!"

With a wild curse, Dusty hurled his body against the steel trap door. But contact only sent a thousand spears of pain coursing through him. And a moment later the roar of mighty engines drowned out his savage words. The crimson doom was moving down the takeoff ramp!

CHAPTER 11
CRIMSON DOOM

UNABLE FOR the moment to grasp the full significance of the plane's motion, Dusty lay sprawled out on the steel floor gasping for breath. Then as realization came to him, he staggered to his feet and braced himself against the wall. Anxiously, he glanced around the dark interior of his sky prison.

At first he could see nothing. But presently his eyes focused on definite objects. However, the objects made the blood run cold in his veins. They formed the top half of the rear wall—long, tapering cylinders of burnished steel, stacked crosswise on top of each other and held in place by metal bands.

One glance at them and he knew that each contained over two hundred pounds of deadly tetalyne! Tetalyne—a newly discovered explosive that made old fashioned TNT seem like a burst of baby firecrackers.

Just how many Tet cylinders there were, he couldn't tell. The darkness of the compartment prevented his counting them all. But there was no need of counting them—the ones he could see were enough to blow half a city into everlasting eternity.

The timing cap of each end had been set at zero. One tap on one of those caps, and all hell would break loose.

He began to make a slow tour of the compartment, hands fobbing smooth walls in an effort to find an exit other than the steel trap upon which he stood.

Suddenly a muffled voice came to his ears. The voice of Fire-Eyes himself! He realized that it was drifting back from a radio speaker in the forward part of the plane.

"Calling all United States stations—calling all United States stations! Stand by for an important message. Stand by for an important message."

During the moment of silence that followed, Dusty darted to the front of the compartment and pressed his ear against the steel wall. When the voice spoke again, it was as clear as though he had phones over his ears.

"This is the commander-in-chief of the Black Invaders speaking. America—your government has refused our terms of peace! We shall now prove to you our power.

"Awake, Americans! Are you to give your blood, and your very lives, for the experimental purposes of those who have set themselves up as your leaders? Are you going to give up your wealth and your homes for dictated ideals that can be nothing else but doomed to failure?

"I pledge you life and happiness beyond your most cherished dreams. But so long as you bend your backs to the yoke of your misguided government, I pledge you nothing but death and destruction!"

The voice clicked off and the compartment was filled with the faint throbbing hum of the four engines atop the wing. Then he heard a second voice—a voice trembling with rage.

"Liar, you lousy baby killer! You'll never win in a hundred thousand years!"

It was the voice of Agent 10. Dusty beat both fists against the steel wall and yelled out.

"Ten—Agent 10, this is Ayres. Can you see where we are headed?"

A gurgling gasp of surprise came back to him.

"You there, Ayres? I thought we'd left you behind!"

DUSTY STARTED to explain, then suddenly checked his words as his groping fingers pressed against something that gave way.

It was a small, four-inch-by-two-inch steel spring panel that ordinarily permitted the exchange of written messages between the bombing officer and the pilot officer. But, by prying it open with his fingers, Dusty could see into the pilot compartment.

He couldn't see either Agent 10 or the President's son. Both were lashed to the wall against which he was pressing, and out of his range of view. But he could see the front of the compartment with its glass windows, one of which had been slid open a half-inch or so.

Below them was the instrument panel, covered with dials and gadgets. And to the right of the panel, the radio-magnetic control unit that operated the plane. Even as he saw it, two of the cylinder magnets moved and he felt the plane respond.

But the thing that caught and held his eyes was the "rep" wheel control not four feet away from him. As though gripped by invisible hands, it was moving a hair this way and then a hair that way, in coordination with the movements of the gyroscopic stabilizer fitted to its base.

Four feet—control of the plane but four feet away from him. God, it could be four million miles.

"Ayres—Ayres? Are you there, man? Can you get in here?"

Agent 10's voice jerked Dusty back from his trance of bitter reverie.

"Listen, 10!" he called out as sudden inspiration came to him, "can you possibly reach that radio control unit on the left with your foot? If you smash it, it will break contact with the radio plane and our controls will go neutral, and we'll fly a straight course until the fuel gives out. It will be impossible for them—"

139

"No can do, Ayres!" the other called back in a groaning voice. "Both the lad and I are tied tighter than hell. Thank God, the kid is still unconscious."

"Then we'll—" began Dusty, and stopped.

"Yes, Ayres!" thickly. "We're headed for Washington, just as he promised. And all my fault. I'm damned sorry."

Dusty tried to make his voice sound cheerful.

"Chin up, we haven't reached there yet. Maybe the boys will shoot us down. Hell, I don't mind—if we can lick them that way!"

"We'll never be shot down, Ayres!" grunted the other. "You know that. You wouldn't do it, yourself, knowing who's aboard."

And then the voice of Fire-Eyes once again crackled out of the radio speaker unit.

"Calling Washington Official, X-34! Calling Washington Official, X-34."

A moment of silence, during which the Washington station must have called back on a wave-length other than the one at which the dial of the bomber's unit was set, and then Fire-Eyes' voice again.

"My personal greeting, X-34! I am sending you three re-minders of your stupidity. One, the President's son, the other a pilot named Ayres, and the third—someone we both know as Agent 10. They are now in a radio bomber, headed for your national capitol.

"The bomber, which is fully loaded with tetalyne, is unes-corted, and you are at liberty to issue orders to shoot it down before it reaches its destination. For your information, the bomber is now about one hundred miles due north of Washington—flying at eighteen thousand feet, and a very easy target."

"That caps it!" came Agent 10's groaning voice, as the speaker unit clicked and went silent. "Dad will be forced to issue the order, but it will never be obeyed."

"Damn it, it's got to be obeyed!" thundered Dusty with conviction he did not feel in his heart. "This ship will blow most of Washington off the map."

"Would you shoot us down, Ayres?"

Dusty didn't answer.

Seconds dragged by, became minutes, but to Dusty, time meant nothing now. He let the wall panel snap back into place, and sank down on the steel floor. There was nothing to do now but wait, and pray that some Yank pilot would steel his heart long enough to plunge down on this ship of crimson doom and send it hurtling down into uninhabited ground.

SUDDENLY A voice crackled harshly out of the speaker unit forward—the voice of the Black Hawk!

"All American stations, stand by! One of your three countrymen, now headed for Washington can save his precious life. There is one parachute aboard that plane. Americans, which two will sacrifice their lives for the third? Americans, which one of the three will save himself?"

For an instant, Dusty was too flabbergasted by the strange message to absorb its complete meaning. And then, like a flash of light, truth blazed a path across his brain. Parachute! He, Dusty, was wearing the vest chute. God, he'd forgotten all about it.

With a roar of rage, he leaped to his feet, clawing at the strap buckles on his back. Damn that rat. His plan was clear now. "Dead men do not suffer—only those who live." Yes, the Hawk had said those words.

And then it happened.

A sharp click and the steel floor fell away. Dusty yelled, flung out his hands to check his fall. But the effort was useless. Like a shot from a gun he went spinning down into brilliant sunshine, head over heels through the air.

The sudden fall sucked the breath from his lungs flattened eyelids against eye-balls, and filled his ears with shrill whining sound. Down, down he rushed, a human meteor tearing earthward.

Mind a spinning blank, it was left for instinct to make his right hand clutch the rip-ring and pull outward. Through windwhipped, watery eyes he saw the pilot chute zip out from in back of him.

Seconds later two billowy clouds of white spewed out, became mushroom shaped, and seemed to jerk his body skyward. And then he was slowly swaying about in a circle, and dangling at the end of double chute shroud lines.

Above him the giant crimson wing was charging through the air. And circling about it, like so many sparrows, was a squadron of Yank pursuit and attack planes.

He saw them, and then lost them as tears of heartaching rage blurred them out.

One of the three would save his life. That's what the American nation had been told. And now he, Dusty Ayres, speed

LIKE A SHOT FROM A GUN HE WENT SPINNING DOWN...

eagle of Uncle Sam's brood, was floating down to everlasting disgrace.

To tell the truth would be wasting words. Neither Agent 10, nor the President's son would live to confirm his story. He, Dusty Ayres, floating down to safety while a brave man and a boy died a horrible death.

Spread out in a panorama of symmetrical beauty was the marble and brick stone city of Washington. But in contrast to the beauty of its buildings, was the panorama of terror in its streets and spring-green parks.

Troops and civilians alike were commandeering every possible means of transportation in one great massed effort to get away from the giant crimson doom that was now circling lower and lower over their heads.

Some anti-aircraft squads remained at their mounted guns, but not one of them dared fire. Not only was the crimson plane a target that no red-blooded American would shoot at, but it was also surrounded with a skyful of American planes.

In a matter of split seconds, Dusty envisioned it all. Then his eye caught a glimpse of the Washington military field off to his right. A plan leaped into his brain.

Throwing up both hands, he grabbed the shroud lines on the right and tugged on them with every atom of his strength. The right chute rebelled for an instant, then caved a bit and he went slipping furiously to the right and down. A few hundred feet above the field he released the folds a bit, and let the chute billow out and check his mad descent. Seconds later, he flexed his legs, and relaxed.

Wham!

He hit the ground with terrific force, and for one awful second he felt as if both legs had been snapped off at the knee. But they hadn't, and gritting his teeth against the pain, he scrambled to his knees, practically tore himself free from the chute vest, and went pounding over to the hangar line.

As he neared it, a dozen figures ran out to him. He swerved and tried to cut past, but the bulky figure of General Horner blocked his path and grabbed him.

"Ayres! Ayres—damn you—you left my son, and that boy up—"

The Intelligence chief never finished. A whirlwind struck out at him, sent him flying, and then that whirlwind roared into the center hangar and into the cockpit of the Silver Flash.

A few gaping mechanics made half-hearted efforts to grab for the wings as twenty-five hundred horses roared into life, and the plane practically leaped out of the hangar.

But those greaseballs might just as well have tried to catch a comet whizzing past. One instant something silvery was before them, and the next they were gawking into each other's faces. DUSTY PULLED the Silver Flash clear and poked its cowled nose straight up for heaven. Up—up he went, straight through the swarm of American planes wheeling and reversing about the slowly circling bomber.

For a split second he flashed a look at the giant wing, started to check his climb, and then cursed and pulled the Silver Flash up steeper.

No, it was useless to try the last part of his plan. The first part had to be taken care of. He had to get the control ship high above him. Once he got it, the bomber's controls would automatically go back to neutral—the gyroscopic stabilizer would do that—and the plane would fly a straight line course to the end of its fuel supply.

Get the radio ship—get the radio ship!

Seconds of hell dragged by. God, where was the control ship? Any minute now, that crimson doom might go roaring down to complete its nation-stunning flight.

A mad bellow burst from his throat. There it was—up there to his left, skimming across a cloud bank. Heeling hard over on wing to the left, he sent the Silver Flash straight down in a wild thundering dive. One thousand feet—two thousand feet—

"Now, old girl!"

The very speed of the ship seemed to tear the words off his lips, as with all his strength, he pulled back on the stick. And, as though it were something really alive and understanding, the plane cut out of its dive and went roaring straight up on its tail—a rocket of chrome steel and dural, careening up into limitless space.

Whether the pilot of that radio plane saw that spear of silver streaking up at him will never be known. But perhaps he did, for a split second later the radio plane curved over and up in a wild climb toward stratosphere safety.

Retreat, however, was the one fatal maneuver to try. Hanging on his prop, Dusty jabbed both thumbs against the electric trigger trips, and sawed rudder. The twin Brownings cowled into the nose did the rest.

Hot singing steel spewed out from the two muzzles, zipped upward and raked the belly of the radio plane from prop to tail wheel. More hot steel slashed into the wing stubs, and traced a chewed-up pattern along the spars.

Perhaps it was five seconds, ten at the most, and then some great invisible fist seemed to crash down on the radio plane. A sea of fire spewed out from its cabin, and a great roar echoed and re-echoed across the heavens.

Like a great bird caught square in the crossfire of the hunters' guns, the plane flopped over on left wing, pivoted crazily for an instant, and then went swirling down leaving behind a long gruesome trail of oily black smoke.

But Dusty didn't see it go down. He only saw the flash of fire. That was enough for him. With a shout of triumph, he kicked the Silver Flash around, tail to the sky, and fed his thundering engine every drop of hop it could take.

Had a falling star raced that plane earthward, it would have been left behind as though tied to the heavens. The engine ceased to thunder out its mighty song of speed and power—it screamed it out in nerve-shattering tone.

Its radio control broken, the bomber had now automatically taken neutral control position, and was flying a straight-ahead course on even keel. Suddenly, Dusty gasped. In the last seconds left him before Dusty's bullets smashed his craft out of the sky, the Black radio plane pilot had set the bomber heading dead on for the Capitol!

It was the last defiant action of a man now dead, and all the fear and terror of a thousand hideous tortures swirled up in

147

Dusty's breast. He pounded the throttle of the Silver Flash until the skin of his hands split, and blood spurted out. But he didn't even feel the pain. Only his brain was alive, and it was on fire, a blazing inferno of jumbled thought fanned to white heat by the hellish picture below.

Out of the corner of his eye he saw a flight of Yank planes swing around and join him in his mad dive earthward. And an instant later his free hand flew out, snapped on the radio switch, and spun the wave-length dial.

"Keep clear—keep clear!" he roared into the transmitter. "Keep clear, you pilots, and give me room!"

Not even bothering to glance back to see if his order was being obeyed, he cut sharply to the left and steepened his dive to the true vertical. The plan that blazed across his brain was nothing more nor less than the plan of a man who wanted to die. But, to him, death meant nothing. God no, if his wild plan failed, death was all he wanted.

Three seconds more—two seconds—one second—now!

Steel fingers curled about the spade grip, pulled the stick back and over to the rear corner. As though actually sensing what was about to take place, the Silver Flash seemed to buck for an instant, and then responded to the will of its master, and went curving up and over.

Tearing one hand from the stick Dusty slammed open the glass cowl and half lifted himself clear. A sea of crimson was directly below him, but he sensed rather than saw it. And then in one continuous motion, he belted the stick back to neutral, hauled back on the throttles and flicked off the ignition switch.

With a swishing moan, the Silver Flash started to keel over slowly, its lower left wing-tips almost touching the glossy stretch of crimson below. Then, as though reluctant to leave, the plane nosed up to the right and dragged its tail across the top of the crimson wing.

IN THAT instant, Dusty braced himself and shot his body downward, arms flung out and fingers clawing frantically.

"So long, old girl!"

Prop wash pulled the words from his throat. A world of crimson rushed up toward him, then crashed into his face. Clawing fingers scratched glassy smoothness. He was on a spinning disc smeared with red grease and sliding off—off into space.

Smack!

The fingers of his right hand slapped against a post. A thousand spears of fire went up his arm and seemed to tear it loose from the shoulder socket. Instinct told him that he had caught hold of one of the stub antenna masts. But he couldn't hold on—momentum was pulling his arm free from his body. He—

The last atom of strength was enough. He got both hands locked about the stub mast, and pulled his body slowly forward. Through relieved eyes he saw the row of windows less than four feet in front of him. A few more seconds—just a few more seconds!

Somehow, he managed to hook numbed legs about the stub mast, coil his muscles and send his body sliding over the airfoil curve of the wing. Cut and bleeding fingers hooked about the window slide groove, jerked it open wide.

Head reeling from the mighty roar of the four engines, eyes blinded by sweat and blood, he tugged and pulled himself down through the narrow opening. For an instant, he stuck, halfway through, and then he went sprawling on his face on the floor of the compartment.

Reeling to his feet, he flung himself into the pilot seat, and grabbed the Dep control. Dully he heard Agent 10 yelling out words of thankfulness. And the next moment they were lost in the hoarse shout that blasted out from his own throat.

A great white dome, topped by a statue, was rushing toward him, and figures like ants were toppling down over the turret railing a frenzied attempt to get clear of the crimson monster thundering straight at them. Their weaving bodies smashed against the curved whiteness, went limp in death, and skidded down out of sight.

A flash panorama—a picture of doom imprinted on the retina of the eye, and then gone forever. But, even as that picture registered, Dusty heeled the Dep wheel over, and thumped his weight down on the rudder pedal.

And in that instant heaven and earth ceased to exist. One hellish split second robbed from time itself while a giant craft of doom seemed to hover motionless in mid-air. Too late—too late—there was not clearance enough for a turn. Crimson doom was going to strike—nothing in the world could stop it now!

Nearer—nearer—

Breath locked in aching lungs, heart skipping beat after beat, and every muscle straining on the controls, Dusty sat rigid, glassy eyes glued to the dome of white.

The wing was going down—the plane was turning—

A wild laugh blasted against his ringing eardrums, and for a precious second he did not realize that the sound came from between his own lips.

A blur of white had swept by, a tremor went through the plane, and then suddenly the broad expanse of sky was in front of him.

"God, Ayres, you did it, lad!"

But Dusty didn't hear the rest of Agent 10's joyful yells, for at that moment something curved down past the crimson wing, through his own heart, it seemed, and on down into oblivion.

His Silver Flash—his one and only sky pal, was hurtling earthward and out of his life forever.

Unashamed tears streaking down his blood and grease-smeared face, he belted the controls savagely, and swung the giant craft around and down toward the military field. Automatically he cranked the wheels down, cut the engines, and floated in to a gentle landing.

An ocean of shouting figures swept across the field and swarmed over the plane. A million questions were roared into his ears, and a million hands grabbed at him, tore at him. He had a dim picture of an ambulance clanging away with the limp figure of the President's son. Another, of Horner throwing both arms about Agent 10.

And then through the sea of swimming, shouting faces, he heard General Horner's voice roaring at him. Big paws clutched him, smothered his face against a tunic front. From way off he heard his own choked voice.

"Gone—best damned ship in the world—gone!"

General Horner's joy-filled, booming reply hammered against his eardrums in vain. For at that moment blessed sleep engulfed him and he went soaring off on a cloud of perfect peace and quiet.

POPULAR PUBLICATIONS
HERO PULPS

LOOK FOR MORE SOON!

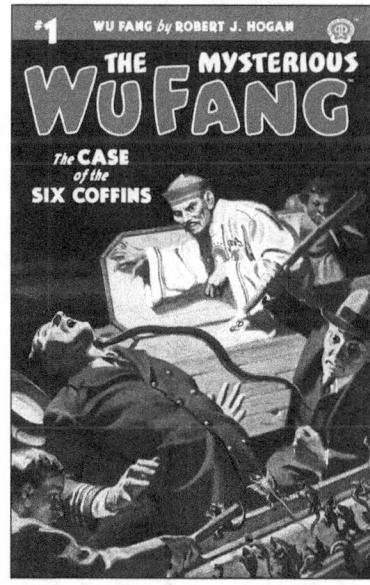